A Legacy of Ghosts

'But d'you know what, Richard? I can almost sense something strange here. I wonder if someone's been coming and going, stealing the pieces one by one?'

Richard was only too willing to believe it. 'I bet they have,' he declared excitedly. 'And I bet they'd take the most valuable things first. They were beautiful ornaments in that cabinet. They were probably worth a fortune!'

The boys exchanged glances. Their eyes were popping. 'The Mackie hoard,' they whispered simultaneously.

'There might be other things missing,' Richard added. 'Oh, if only we could get in there!'

A crafty half-smile crept over Ben's face. 'How do we know we can't?'

A LEGACY OF GHOSTS

Colin Dann

RED FOX

For Bill and Penny and family

A Red Fox Book

Published by Random House Children's Books
20 Vauxhall Bridge Road, London SW1V 2SA

A division of Random House UK Ltd

London Melbourne Sydney Auckland
Johannesburg and agencies throughout the world

First published in 1991 by
Hutchinson Children's Books
Red Fox edition 1992
Reprinted 1992, 1993

Printed and bound in Great Britain by
Cox & Wyman Ltd, Reading, Berkshire

ISBN 0 09 986540 8

Contents

— 1 —
The House of the Martins

There had been rumours for years about the wealth of old Mr Mackie. People called it 'old Mackie's Hoard'. Some said it was treasure – gold or precious stones – and some said it was money – all in notes, and hidden away somewhere. No one in Hallenden knew anything positive about it and no one was sure how the rumours had started. But there seemed always to have been rumours and people made up their own minds whether they believed them or not. Mr Mackie himself was not a friendly man and rarely spoke to anyone unless he had to. At the end of his life he was housebound, his only company a thin white cat and a rather drab housekeeper who came in every day to look after all his wants. The housekeeper's name was Mrs Crisp and it was she who found Mr Mackie dead in his bed one summer morning. He was eighty-two and had no relatives. She had often referred to him as 'the last of his line'. After contacting the doctor and the solicitor Mrs Crisp felt there was no more for her to do and, later that morning when the doctor had called, she had left the house and never entered it again.

Everything was left just as it had been during Mr

Mackie's life. Not a cup, not a stick of furniture was moved. The only thing that was taken out of the house was Mr Mackie himself. He had been a huge man and it needed six men to carry the heavy coffin with a seventh one walking alongside to steady it as necessary. The cat disappeared. There were no mourners.

The nearest house to Mr Mackie's was where the Bright family lived. Geoffrey Bright owned the hardware shop in Hallenden on the Kent/Sussex borders. His wife Valerie helped in the shop during school hours when business demanded it. They had two children, Richard who was twelve and Virginia, ten. On the day of the funeral, which was in August, Geoffrey Bright closed his shop at one o'clock. It was early-closing day in Hallenden. As he walked home he saw Mr Todd the solicitor, whom he knew, hurrying along the High Street in his direction. He was wearing a black arm-band. They stopped for a moment to exchange a word.

'I hope nothing – ' Mr Bright began.

'No, no. A client's funeral,' Mr Todd said hastily. 'Old Mackie.'

'Really! I didn't know he had been ill?'

'He hadn't. It was simply old age. I've got his house to deal with – and everything else.'

'How do you mean?'

'No surviving relatives. He left his entire estate to charity. Some unknown organization down in Wales. They want me to sell everything. The house should fetch a good price. The contents will have to go by auction. I'm sorry – I can't stop. I think I may be late. Goodbye.'

'Oh – goodbye.' Mr Bright's thoughts turned immediately to 'the hoard'. He wondered if the rumours might at last be substantiated. Later he gave the news to his wife who was at home because of the school holidays.

She was watching for his stocky, sandy-haired figure from the window. A cold lunch was on the table awaiting his arrival.

'Come on, children! Daddy's here,' she called as he came through the door.

'I've just seen Todd,' he told her. 'Old Mackie's dead. House to be sold and everything in it. Some odd charity's going to get the Mackie hoard.'

They talked about it over the meal-table. Richard's eyes roved from his little dark-haired mother to his father and back again, drinking in the conversation. The subject fascinated him. There had always been a mystery about the Mackie house – the 'House of the Martins' as he liked to call it – because every summer a throng of the little birds built their cupped nests there under the eaves. He and his friend Ben Tompkins used to make up stories about the place. They pretended it was haunted and that there was buried treasure in the garden. He looked at his sister. Ginny was intent on her meal, not a flicker of interest in her blue eyes. Richard gobbled at his food, aching to be off to tell Ben what he had heard.

'Don't bolt your lunch like that,' Mrs Bright cautioned him. 'You'll have indigestion.'

'Is Richard greedy?' Ginny enquired lazily, pushing a hand through her thick blonde hair and swinging her legs under the table.

'No, he's not greedy; just hasty,' her father answered. He glanced at Richard. 'You must have been hungry?'

'Starving,' Richard muttered and glared at Ginny. The children had quite different temperaments and were not often playmates. Also they didn't resemble one another in appearance and a stranger would never have taken them for brother and sister. While Ginny was blonde and fair-skinned, Richard was dark-haired, dark-eyed and had a skin that tanned very easily to a glowing golden brown. In this he took after his mother.

The meal was soon over. 'Can I go out?' Richard asked promptly. 'Ben's coming over.'

'Of course,' said his mother. 'Are you taking your bikes?'

'Yes.'

'Mind how you go. No larking about.'

'No, Mum.' Richard dashed away to fetch his bike which was leaning against the laburnum tree in the garden. It was a new bigger bike, painted a bright cheerful red, which he was getting used to after out-growing his old one. Ben's bike was similar. The two boys were growing fast and both were tall for their age. They greeted each other at the gate. Richard gave a wave to his parents who were watching from the window. Then the friends pedalled furiously away, racing each other.

'Not much good, your cautioning words,' Mr Bright muttered to his wife. 'Why does he always have to tear about so?'

Mrs Bright smiled affectionately. 'Just high spirits,' she said.

'He's only showing off,' Virginia said in her clear precise voice.

Ben Tompkins was what Geoffrey Bright called a 'harum scarum' lad. He always seemed to be getting into scrapes at school, but shrugged them all off as if nothing was of much importance except enjoying himself. He was a very lively, intelligent boy, who wasted some of his abilities by playing pranks to make his classmates laugh. His face was covered with freckles and usually wore a mischievous smile. He had a crop of coppery hair and dancing grey eyes. Mr and Mrs Bright had some qualms about Richard's friendship with Ben but it was impossible not to like the boy. He was always polite and interesting even if his impudent smile sometimes seemed a little mocking. His father was a bank manager in Hallenden and he had a beautiful older sister called Angela whom Richard admired tremendously.

Ben always talked a lot and it was a while before Richard could silence him long enough to tell him his news. 'Listen, Ben. Listen!'

Ben's chatter ceased abruptly and he looked open-mouthed at Richard, pretending to be dumbfounded at being shouted at.

'You know the House of the Martins?'

Of course he did, it was only a couple of hundred metres from the Brights' house.

'Well, it's empty. Mr Mackie's dead. Shall we go and look in and see if we can see anything?'

'See what? The hoard?' Ben joked.

'No, don't be silly. But we might see *something* – you know, something interesting.'

Ben agreed. He was really as curious about the place as Richard was. Richard led the way and they cycled up to the house which was open at the front to the road. It was built of dark brick. It was broad and double-fronted with a pillared porch and heavy latticed windows. It had a distinctly gloomy appearance. There was a long garden at the back, dark with greatly overgrown shrubs and holly bushes. No gardener had been near the place in years and the lawn was like a meadow. At the house end there was a short flight of steps leading down to an unpainted door under the house. They took their bikes round the back and laid them down on the ground. In the garden there was a small, broken shed, half buried under a lilac tree and, in the adjoining field, they saw a dilapidated brick construction which had been used as an air-raid shelter during the War.

'Did you ever see *him*?' Ben asked as they crept towards a window.

'Only once or twice. He sometimes stood looking out at the street at the front.'

'I wonder what he was like?'

'Enormous,' Richard answered innocently. 'Like a giant, with bushy grey hair.'

'No, I mean what sort of person was he?'

'No one knows, do they? My father never spoke to him but he knows he used to own an antiques shop. That must have been how he made all his money.' It was clear the 'hoard' was very much a reality in Richard's mind.

'My father said he was a miser,' Ben rejoined. 'He didn't use the bank. Said he didn't trust them. He used to pay for everything with cash.'

'I don't see why that makes him a miser,' Richard murmured, looking puzzled. Ben giggled.

The windows were stained and dirty. Ben rubbed at one with his sleeve. They pressed their noses to it and peered in. Over their heads the house-martins flitted to and fro, uttering their little high-pitched clicks and chirrups. Every now and then one would alight on its nest and push its way through the tiny entrance, bringing a morsel of food for the nestlings inside.

'What a jumble of objects,' Ben remarked. 'It looks a bit like an antiques shop in *there*.'

'It does, doesn't it? I suppose he collected things,' said Richard. 'I bet some of them are valuable.'

''Spect so,' Ben murmured. 'Look at that sideboard. It's gigantic.'

'This must be the dining-room,' said Richard.

'Oh, you are clever,' Ben mocked him playfully. Richard grinned.

They moved round the house, staring in at each room:

kitchen, sitting-room, study. Every room was crammed full of things – heavy furniture, curios, ornaments, clocks, paintings, old weapons, a globe – in a sort of organized clutter. The study had shelves of books, many of them leatherbound.

'I wonder what'll happen to it all?' Ben mused. 'I'd love to go in there and explore. You never know what you might find.'

'It's all going to be sold, my father says.'

'Sold? Who'd buy all that lot?'

'I dunno. Different people, I s'pose.'

'My father likes old books,' said Ben. 'He may be interested in some of those.'

'You can just imagine old Mackie sitting in that great low armchair, reading through his books,' Richard said. 'He never went out, you know. He must have read all day long. I bet he read every single one of those lots of times.'

'Didn't he ever eat?' Ben laughed.

'Of course he did. But he had a book open on the table the whole time,' Richard invented. 'And he never spoke. Not to anyone, except his housekeeper.'

'I don't expect he slept much,' said Ben. 'He couldn't have got tired very easily if he never did anything. I expect he read half the night, sitting up in bed.'

'A four-poster,' Richard claimed, getting into the spirit of the game.

'In a nightcap and – and – a silk dressing-gown,' Ben hazarded.

'By candlelight, of course,' said Richard.

'With a blunderbuss under the bed,' Ben affirmed.

They laughed together and the game developed with all sorts of unlikely images and scenes, the boys' imaginations running riot. It wasn't difficult to invent all sorts of stories about old Mackie, his hoard and the House of the Martins, and the boys tried to cap each other's tales with something even more grotesque or far-fetched. They didn't know their games fell far short of the real adventure that was soon to befall them in that gloomy deserted building.

— 2 —
A Face at the Window

The garden of the House of the Martins became a regular venue for Richard and Ben. They played hide-and-seek in the rank grass, hunted for creepy-crawlies and sometimes just lay in the sunshine, watching the birds and insects flitting about, and inventing more elaborate yarns about Mr Mackie's way of life. Every so often they would wander over to the house and look in, trying to spot a new object – a piece of china, a horse brass, a vase – in the museum-like interior that they hadn't noticed before. They became quite knowledgeable about the contents. They had the place to themselves and felt they knew more about it than anyone. Nobody but they seemed to show any interest in it – even their parents weren't aware how much time they spent there. Then one day they got a real surprise. It was very hot and the two boys were lazily tossing a cricket ball to each other, practising difficult catches. Ben was facing the house and was just about to bowl the ball over, his arm raised. Richard saw him suddenly jump, quite involuntarily. A startled look came over his face.

'Richard!' hissed Ben. 'Look!'

Richard was already swinging round, following Ben's gaze. A dark face was staring out at them from the dining-room. The boys hardly had time to register this appearance, let alone mark the features, before it vanished. It was just like an apparition. The friends were shaken and they slipped quickly out of the garden without even remembering to pick up their bikes.

Once safely away they began to chatter excitedly. Had someone come to live there? Or was it a burglar? Who could it be? Where would he have got in? It wasn't long, of course, before they realized they had left their bikes behind and would have to go back for them. 'You lead,' Ben tittered.

Richard's habitually earnest expression hardened. He looked very determined. 'O.K. Come on.'

They were both a little scared, yet at the same time keen to find an explanation for the strange face. They quickly noticed the front door was still shut and that none of the windows had been forced. They crept round to the back to retrieve their bikes, treading carefully. There was no further sign of anyone. Their confidence returned. Richard actually went up to the dining-room window to look for evidence. There was none there, nor in any of the other rooms. It was almost as if they had imagined the whole thing.

The friends looked at one another, puzzled. 'There was a face,' Ben said doubtfully, 'wasn't there? We can't have dreamt it, we *both* saw it.'

'There was someone there all right,' Richard confirmed. 'He must have left again before we came back.' But he didn't sound as if he had convinced himself.

'Suppose the face comes back again?' Ben suggested. He couldn't quite accept that it was a person.

Richard shrugged. 'So what? We're not doing any harm.'

'But if someone else *has* come to live here, we can't go on playing in this garden.'

'No. But we don't know that yet. I'd love to find out.'

'So would I,' said Ben. 'Let's see if our parents know anything.'

Later on they both sounded out their fathers. Mr Tompkins, the bank manager, knew nothing about it. 'You and that house,' he said. 'I know you and Richard are fascinated by it. But please, don't start imagining things.'

'We didn't imagine it!'

'Well, perhaps it was Mr Todd's clerk. *I* don't know.'

Geoffrey Bright was equally dismissive. 'No sale could have gone through that quickly,' he remarked in answer to Richard's chatter. 'Besides, even if the house had been sold, nobody could move in with the old boy's possessions still intact. Are you sure it wasn't Mr Todd? He must be the only one with a key.'

'Of course I'm sure,' said Richard. And that's how the subject was left just then.

Richard and Ben returned to the House of the Martins regularly over the next few days, hoping for another sighting to dispel their growing uncertainty. They saw no further signs.

'I wish we could get inside, ourselves,' said Ben. 'Then we'd be able to look properly.'

'We still might not find anything,' Richard murmured, glancing for the twentieth time around the Mackie sitting-room, his serious face next to Ben's lively one pressed against the window. 'Wait a moment, though,' he suddenly whispered. 'I don't believe it! Ben, Ben!' he spluttered. 'Look at the globe. It's been moved! And – and – the cabinet! Some of the china's gone!'

Ben flattened his face still further against the pane. 'You're right,' he cried. 'That cabinet was full of ornaments. Wow! There must be five or six missing.' Then he added in a distinctly disappointed tone, 'But no, it can't mean anything except that the solicitor's sold them off.'

Richard was crestfallen. But all at once he perked up. 'That can't be it, Ben,' he said. 'My father specifically mentioned there was to be an auction – you know, of everything. So the things couldn't be sold off bit by bit. Could they?'

'I don't know.' Ben shook his head. 'You may be right. I don't know enough about it. But d'you know what, Richard? I can almost sense something strange here. I wonder if someone's been coming and going, stealing the pieces one by one?'

Richard was only too willing to believe it. 'I bet they have,' he declared excitedly. 'And I bet they'd take the most valuable things first. They were beautiful ornaments in that cabinet. They were probably worth a fortune!'

The boys exchanged glances. Their eyes were popping. 'The Mackie hoard,' they whispered simultaneously.

'There might be other things missing,' Richard added. 'Oh, if only we could get in there!'

A crafty half-smile crept over Ben's face. 'How do we know we can't?'

Richard gazed at him. 'How do you mean?'

'Well we've never actually tried, have we?'

'No,' Richard breathed. 'We haven't. D'you think – '

'I think we should try,' said Ben. 'Try all the windows and all the doors we can reach.' His grey eyes sparkled with excitement. 'After all, there must be a way in, mustn't there? We know that now.'

They wasted no time. They began on the garden side, moved round to the front, trying the kitchen door on the way. They tested the front door and every window fastening. They found everything shut tight. But Ben wasn't about to give up.

'What about a key?' he suggested. 'Sometimes people hide a key under a mat – or – somewhere.'

They went back to the front porch. There was a doormat. They lifted it. There was nothing underneath. They looked through the letter-box in case one was hanging from a piece of string. Then they looked in and under a stone pot which stood by the porch. Eventually they ran out of places to search but they had found no key.

Richard scratched his dark head, looking about for ideas. 'What about that old shed?' he asked.

'Of course, yes. Well done,' Ben responded. 'That was a brainwave.'

They ran to the lilac tree and bent under its unpruned branches.

The shed door opened easily but with an accentuated creak as if it were complaining. Inside was a hotchpotch of garden tools, jars, boxes and other paraphernalia. And there, directly at eye-level, was a long key hanging on a hook. The boys' excitement was tremendous. They jostled each other, both trying to grab it at once. Richard laughed and allowed his friend to take it.

'It must be the front door key,' he said.

'Of course it isn't,' Ben said scathingly. 'How could this fit a Yale lock?' He brandished the key which had specks of rust on it. 'And it'd hardly be left in here, would it?'

'O.K., know-all. Where does it fit?'

'The kitchen door, I should think. Come on, what are we waiting for?'

It didn't fit the kitchen door, neither did it fit the french windows leading to the dining-room. The boys were stumped.

'There must be another door,' said Richard.

'Only that one under the house,' Ben returned. 'You know, by the steps.' They had never ventured down there.

'That should be it then,' said Richard.

They scampered down the steps. Ben slid the key into the lock and turned it. They held their breath. There was a click. Ben grasped the door-handle and pushed hard. The door opened a little and then stuck fast. They could see it was pitch-dark inside. Ben hesitated.

'We don't have to go in there, do we?' he said. 'I mean – we wouldn't see anything.'

Richard was a little scared too but he tried not to show it. 'We could at least try the door again. Push together. I bet it hasn't been opened for years. It would let some light in and we might be able to see a bit.'

'All right,' said Ben, trying not to appear faint-hearted.

They put their shoulders to the door and gave it a good shove. It burst open and, as they almost fell in after it, they heard a hurried scuttling noise as though someone was hastening to run away. The boys sprang back alarmed and leapt up the steps. In that brief moment in the dim light they had caught just a glimpse of what was obviously the cellar of the house and which had been used for storage. It was stacked with boxes and all sorts of containers. At the top of the steps the boys paused. They felt foolish and were angry with themselves. They were dying to know what had caused the noise.

'There's something in there anyway,' said Ben as he recovered his composure.

'Rats, I should think.'

'Sounded too heavy for that.'

'We could fetch a torch.'

'Yes, let's. I'll go,' volunteered Ben. 'I'll be as quick as I can.' He ran towards his bike. 'You stay here on guard,' he called behind him, 'to see if anything comes out.' He was on his way before Richard could protest. Richard kept well back from the top of the steps. He was ready for flight in a second. But he kept his eyes on the open door.

He saw nothing. A bit later he glanced at his watch. He was proud of this. It had been an expensive present from his father. He realized it was approaching the time when he had to be home for supper. He also noticed his leather watch-strap was badly frayed and threatened to break away. He made a mental note to tell his father he needed a new one. In just a few minutes Ben was back. He was carrying a square battery lamp which he held up with a flourish.

'This has a really powerful beam,' he announced. 'We'll be able to see right into the cellar without having to go inside.'

Richard was content. He followed Ben down the steps. Ben switched on the lamp and shone it all round the cellar. They saw nothing more unusual than empty bottles and cartons, some unopened boxes, a wine-rack with a couple of bottles still in it, a pile of sacks and some broken glasses. There was a sharp smell of coaldust.

'Disappointing,' said Ben, though secretly relieved there had been no nasty surprises lurking within.

'I've got to get back,' said Richard. 'We can explore another time.'

'Yes,' said Ben. 'It's getting late. We could come back tomorrow morning?'

'O.K. And I'll bring a torch too.'

They pulled the door closed. After the initial wrenching it now came smoothly without any hitch. They locked it and replaced the key in the shed. They began to feel very brave now that they knew they didn't have to prove themselves until the next day.

'There could be all sorts of things living down there amongst that rubbish,' said Ben lightly. 'I can't wait to find out.'

'I hope no one gets there before us.' He began to whistle faintly, thinking of his tea.

—3—
The Cellar

Valerie Bright began filling the washing machine soon after breakfast. Ginny was getting under her feet. Her mother was glad to see Richard was hoping to go out. He had put on old clothes.

'Is Ben coming?' she asked him.

'Er – sort of,' Richard replied. 'We're meeting up anyway, if that's all right?'

'Of course. Look, dear,' Mrs Bright straightened up, 'you couldn't take Ginny with you this morning, could you? I know you don't like to, when you're with Ben, but she's really getting on my nerves.'

'*I* don't want to play with Ben,' Virginia said superciliously. 'He's not my friend.'

Richard pulled a face at her. 'Do I have to, Mum? What can we do when Ginny's with us? She'll spoil everything. And she doesn't want to come anyway.'

Mrs Bright sighed. 'All right. But don't be late for lunch. I've got to help your father in the shop this afternoon. He's terribly busy. So you'll have to stay here with Ginny whether you like it or not. Now mind what I say.'

'I won't be late, I promise,' Richard said with relief.

'Why have you got all your old togs on?' his mother asked incidentally.

'Oh, we thought – um – we might play football,'

Richard extemporized. He looked down at his old T-shirt and jeans. He didn't want any tell-tale coaldust on clean clothes.

'Off you go then.' Mrs Bright turned to Ginny who was pulling the pile of washing about. 'Ginny, for Heaven's sake, can't you find something else to do?'

'No,' Ginny answered cheekily. 'I'm bored.'

'*Are* you? Well, I'll soon find something to occupy you!'

It was a cool day with a gusting wind. Richard left the house with his father's spare torch tucked out of sight under his jacket. He got to the House of the Martins before Ben and went straight to the shed to fetch the cellar key. Ben soon arrived. He was also wearing different clothes but it was obvious they were clean on that morning. Richard looked him up and down. Ben realized he wasn't dressed for the occasion. And he'd forgotten his torch.

'Oh dear,' he said. 'I haven't really come prepared, have I?'

'Doesn't look like it.'

'It'll probably be filthy down there.'

For a fleeting moment Richard wondered if Ben was deliberately trying to avoid going into the cellar but he brushed the thought aside. Ben wasn't like that.

'D'you want to go home and change?'

'No. Never mind. I'll just have to be careful. You can go first.'

'Thanks,' Richard said ironically.

They went to the cellar door, unlocked it again and pushed it open. This time there wasn't a sound from inside. Richard flipped his torch on and stepped in. The floor felt gritty under his feet. He took another step, casting the beam of the torch around. The walls and ceiling were festooned with cobwebs and grime. There

were stacks of empty wine-cases. There were also some
that hadn't been touched.

'Phew,' Richard whistled. 'Old Mackie must've been
quite a boozer.'

The boys went further in. In one spot there were
remnants of a supply of coal. On the right-hand wall
was a closed door to what looked like a cupboard. They
didn't bother with that but edged forward towards some
discarded and very ancient-looking pieces of furniture.
As they stopped again there came a sudden bang. The
cellar door had slammed shut behind them. They
grasped each other, frightened, and waited. There was no
other noise except the moaning of the wind through a
crack under the door. They began to breathe more freely.

'It was the wind,' said Richard. 'It's blown the door
shut.'

'I thought it was someone trying to lock us in,' Ben said.

'So did I. Come on, we'd better go and see if we can
get out again.'

They retraced their steps and Richard shone his torch
on the door. 'Oh no!' he cried. 'There's no handle on
the inside. The door's quite smooth.'

'Pull it,' Ben urged. 'At the edge.'

'No, it's no good. It won't budge. It's shut fast.'

'There must be another way out.'

'Must there? I hope you're right, Ben. Otherwise . . .'
Richard didn't finish.

'We didn't go right to the end,' said Ben. 'We ought
to look there.'

They turned about and went back to where some old
chairs and a chest or two were standing. Richard shone
the torch at the far end of the cellar and, with cries of
relief, the boys saw a flight of steps which appeared to
lead up to the inside of the house. They made straight
for them, not stopping to examine anything else.

'I wonder where we shall come out?' Richard murmured as they began to ascend. 'We'd better be careful.'

At the top of the steps there was a trap-door with a handle in the centre. Richard hesitated. Then suddenly the friends heard noises, not from above but distant and from below where they had paused. Richard hastily pushed the trap-door which opened on a hinge. The boys emerged into the house itself which was quiet and empty. They found they were in the hall, by the stairwell. They strained to catch the noise beneath them. It was a kind of regular, hollow echo and it was coming nearer.

'It sounds like footsteps,' Richard whispered. 'But . . . but how can it be?'

'Shut the door,' Ben said sharply. 'I don't think we should stay here.' He clutched Richard's arm. 'It's ghostly!'

Richard closed the trap-door with a thud and the friends ran to the front of the house, into the sitting-room. Ben opened a window and was up on the dark oak windowsill in a trice. Richard followed. They clambered through and jumped into the garden. Richard pushed the window to, behind them. They sprinted round to the side for their bikes. Just as they were about to leave, Richard let out a wail.

'What is it?' Ben sounded on edge.

'My watch,' moaned Richard. 'I've lost my watch.'

'Lost it! Where?'

'I don't know. I'm sure I had it on when we went into the cellar. Oh hell! I must have dropped it in the house!' He looked at Ben, appealing.

The prospect of having to go back inside turned rapidly from a feeling of anxiety to one of anger in Ben's case. 'Dropped it! How could you possibly have dropped it?' he demanded. 'You don't carry your watch in your hand.'

'No, it's the strap. It must have broken. I meant to . . . Ohh!' Richard wailed again. 'I must go back for it, Ben. Will you come with me?'

'I don't see why I should just because . . .'

'Please, Ben. Please. I don't feel like going back in there alone.'

Ben looked at his friend sullenly. All he wanted to do just then was to get away but he knew he couldn't let Richard down. 'Did you drop it in the house?' he asked at length. 'I don't mind going back that far.'

'I don't know,' Richard answered. 'I think I probably did.'

'Come on then. Let's get it over with.'

They left their bikes by the front fence. Richard tugged the window open again from outside. They climbed up, after first hunting under the window. Inside the sitting-room they held themselves quite still, listening for the echoes. From there they could hear nothing. They began to search, covering their steps back to the trap-door. The watch was nowhere to be seen. They paused under the stairwell. Ben looked grim.

'I'm sorry,' he said, trying to ignore Richard's helpless expression. 'I'm not going down into the cellar. I've already got these clothes dirty. My mother will go mad. And anyway,' he added lamely, 'I haven't got a torch.'

Richard knew perfectly well these were just excuses. 'I can't blame you,' he said. 'I don't fancy it myself with those echoes . . .'

Ben tried to make amends. 'I'll go and look around the garden, if you like,' he offered. 'You never know, it may be by the steps where we started off.'

'I'm sure it isn't,' Richard said hopelessly.

'Worth a try.'

Of course the watch wasn't found, although they

combed the area. Ben looked awkward. 'I – I'd better go, Richard,' he said.

'Yes.' Richard's face was miserable. 'You can do one thing for me. Tell me what time it is. I've got to be back to look after Ginny.'

Ben glanced at his own watch. 'Half past eleven,' he said.

'Thanks,' said Richard. He showed no signs of moving.

Ben hesitated. 'You're not thinking of going into the cellar again, are you?'

'Doubt it.'

'Good. You ought to wait until we can both go. I'll put old clothes on next time.'

'When will that be?'

'Well . . . tomorrow? It'd be better to leave it for a bit, wouldn't it?'

'S'pose so. You mean – the noises?'

'Yes.'

'All right then. I'll see you.'

Ben was relieved. 'What time?'

'I dunno. Any time. I'll give you a ring.'

Ben got on his bike. 'See you.' He began to pedal away.

Richard stood irresolute. He really couldn't make up his mind whether to risk continuing his search. He told himself it might only take a minute or two. The watch could be just inside the trap-door at the top of the interior steps. Then he could be in and out in a flash. But, once Ben had disappeared, he felt less courageous than before. He didn't know how he'd explain the loss to his parents. He sauntered over to the sitting-room window. He looked puzzled. It didn't appear to be at quite the same angle as he had left it. He gave it a tentative tug. It didn't move. The window was closed!

Richard jumped back. His heart pounded. There *was* someone in the house.

His first thought was to run but, despite himself, he was very curious. When could that window have been closed? Only while he and Ben had been searching the garden. With a start Richard realized that now they couldn't get back into the cellar and he wouldn't be able to retrieve his watch. He groaned out loud: 'Oh no. It's really lost now.' He tramped around the outside of the house, looking into all the rooms in case there was just some simple explanation for the window such as the solicitor or Mrs Crisp entering the house in the normal way and finding it unfastened. But neither Mr Todd nor Mrs Crisp were in evidence as Richard soon discovered. No, he knew who had fastened that window. The owner of that dark face who had looked out at him and Ben playing in the garden!

All at once Richard recalled that the cellar door wasn't locked. It had blown shut behind them and so therefore could still be opened from the outside. They had left the key in the lock. So, unless someone else had locked it . . . Richard thought of his precious watch and hastened at once to the cellar door to check. The key was still there. Richard pocketed it. Now he and Ben could always re-enter whenever they wished. He sat on one of the steps and thought. If the unknown person had entered the house without their knowing, why couldn't he – Richard – enter it now without *his* knowing? He would need to use extreme caution, but the possibility remained. He wondered what the time was. If he was going to make a move it would have to be soon. His mother's instructions echoed in his head.

Richard wavered. On the one hand he pictured himself nipping into the cellar, finding his watch easily and making his escape without mishap. How proud and happy he would feel if he could sit at lunch, reliving in his own mind his daring solo dash. But on the other hand . . . supposing it didn't work out like that and he came up against that unknown somebody. He simply couldn't decide. The minutes passed. He imagined his mother already looking for his return, her patience ebbing fast. And then, on top of that, his admission of guilt and carelessness about his watch. Richard was on tenter-hooks, his mind flitting from one likely scenario to the other.

At last, more to put himself out of his misery than anything else, he stood up and crept down to the cellar door. He put his hand on the knob. He turned it very slowly and, even more slowly, pushed it open, listening hard all the while. There were no strange echoes, no sounds now of any kind. He carefully wedged the door with the corner of a box. He flicked the switch on his torch. Then he tiptoed inside. It all seemed quiet and safe. Richard renewed his search, concentrating on the grimy floor.

He reached the interior steps again. There were no alarms but also no trace of his watch. He looked for it on the steps themselves but there was no joy for him there either. He went back once more over the gritty cellar floor in case he had missed anything. Now he did make a discovery, but not of his watch. The door in the wall he and Ben had taken for a cupboard door was wide open. And it opened on to no cupboard. Instead, what was revealed was a low dark passage leading off underground. Richard was enormously excited. The hand holding his torch trembled. He was a little scared but nonetheless exultant. Here was the answer to the mysterious noises, the echoes and even the face at the window. For here was another entrance to the House of the Martins that was being used by someone else.

—4—
The Stranger

Richard could hardly contain himself over lunch. He hadn't dared to explore the secret passage by himself but he was only waiting for his mother to leave before he got on the phone to Ben. The missing watch hadn't been mentioned. He had decided to keep quiet about it unless he was challenged, hoping that he might somehow rescue it before his parents had noticed its loss.

At last Mrs Bright got herself ready. She darted about, clearing the table, making herself up, changing into her shop clothes, seeming to do all three at once. These hurried little bursts of movement and activity were very characteristic. Her husband often remarked that she seemed to do everything on the run. Her dark little figure bustled about from room to room. 'Right, children, I'm going. Now do try not to irritate each other. I'll be back by five. Richard, you're in charge so don't go wandering off. If you want to play in the garden make sure you lock the kitchen door and keep the key safe. Ginny, try to look a bit more cheerful, love.' She rushed out of the door.

Virginia hadn't yet recovered from a fit of sulking brought on by the dusting her mother had given her to do as a way of keeping her occupied. 'I suppose you want to do something boring like playing cricket,' she said to Richard.

'No,' said Richard. 'You can play on your own. I'm going to talk to Ben.'

'You're supposed to be looking after me,' Ginny said provokingly, 'not making telephone calls.'

Richard ignored her. Ben was soon listening to the details of Richard's discovery. He let out a whoop of exhilaration. 'We *must* investigate,' he said at once. 'When can you go back?'

'Not today,' Richard told him. 'I've got Ginny with me. Mum's at work, as I said before. Isn't it infuriating?'

Ben was silent for a moment. Thoughts raced through his mind. Then he said, 'That face we saw – whoever it was has been stealing from the house.'

'That's what I think,' Richard agreed. 'I bet he stole those china pieces. We could try to track him down.'

It sounded very daring. Ben said: 'The first thing to do is to find where that tunnel leads to. I say, Richard, this is becoming a real adventure.'

Richard rang off, having arranged to meet the next day. Virginia had been listening to every word, trying to guess what he and Ben had been talking about. She hated her brother's habit of keeping things from her.

'I heard you,' she said emphatically, 'so you've got to tell me what it was all about.'

Richard was annoyed. 'I might have guessed you'd be eavesdropping,' he grumbled. 'Anyway, if you heard me, you know it all already.'

'I don't know it!' Ginny cried, exasperated. 'Something about a passage. I bet it was that house you were talking about: the House of the Martins.'

'What if it was?'

Ginny was intrigued despite herself. 'Oh, tell me

about it, Rich,' she wheedled. 'Please. You always try to leave me out.'

'You're not old enough,' Richard told her with a superior air.

'Of course I'm old enough. You only have to tell me,' she spluttered, infuriated.

Richard was silent.

'I'll tell Mummy where you've been,' Ginny threatened.

Richard shrugged. 'She knows we play there anyway. What's the harm? It's empty.'

'She doesn't know about your watch,' Ginny said subtly, a sly smile creeping over her face. 'I'll tell her you've lost it.'

'I haven't lost it,' Richard blustered, 'it's . . . it's just gone missing.'

'Same thing. I heard you say to Ben you hadn't found it, so there.'

'Oh, you *are* a pest,' Richard said angrily. 'All right, I'll tell you. Ben and I discovered a cellar under the house. We went in there to look around and there's – um – a passage running off it.'

Ginny looked at him suspiciously. She knew this wasn't the whole story. 'Is that where you lost your watch?'

'Must've been, yes.'

'Shall you and I go and look for it?'

'Certainly not!' Richard told her at once. 'We're not to go further than our garden. You heard Mum.'

'She wouldn't know,' Ginny whispered. Her eyes were dancing with anticipation. 'She'll be gone hours. You could just show me this cellar, anyway, and then we'll come back.'

'No!' Richard exclaimed hotly. 'And that's final.'

'Oh!' Ginny wailed her disappointment. 'Why are you

so rotten to me?' Then she changed her tack. 'Right then. I *shall* tell Mum – and Dad – about your watch. They'll be ever so cross,' she added spitefully.

Richard seethed. 'Oh, you – you nuisance!' he shouted. But he knew he was beaten. And so did Virginia, who was grinning from ear to ear at his dilemma.

'Shall I put my old jeans on?' she asked cheekily.

'Yes, yes, hurry up. We'll have to be quick. And Ginny – you wait. I'll get my own back for this.'

Ginny stuck her tongue out at her brother and ran upstairs. Richard led his sister out of the kitchen door, locked it and put the key in his pocket. As he did so he found the other key there – the Mackie cellar key – and suddenly he had an idea. He left his bike behind and took Ginny's hand as they went along the road. Ginny hated this.

'I'm not a baby,' she insisted, struggling to free herself.

Richard pulled her after him. He meant to go through the motions of taking her to the house and then pretend he'd lost the key. They reached it with Ginny still vainly twisting her hand. Richard took her round to the back garden.

'*I* can't see what's so special about it,' she muttered, looking up at the building. 'Where's the cellar?'

'Down here.' They went down the steps. 'The key's gone!' Richard exclaimed in his best imitation of surprise.

Ginny looked up at him sullenly, suspecting a trick. 'What key?'

'The cellar key,' said Richard. 'You can't get in without it. It was here in the lock. Someone must have removed it.'

'Oh yes? Who would do that? I don't believe you.'

'I'm afraid you'll have to, Ginny. I can't show you the cellar now.'

'Oh, you beast, Richard!' Ginny stamped her foot. 'I know you're fibbing. You know where the key is all the time. You and Ben are going to come here tomorrow. I heard you say so.'

'That was before I found it locked.'

'How do you know it's locked? You haven't even tried,' Ginny berated her brother. She grabbed the door-handle and wrestled with it. Of course it wouldn't budge. 'It's not fair!' she shrilled. 'I can tell you're fibbing. You play with Ben but you never want to with me.' She sounded so upset Richard actually began to waver. After all, what would it matter? He could open it up, show her the dark cellar, and then they would go home. He hadn't brought the torch so they couldn't go far inside. It would keep Ginny quiet and she'd have to make a pact with him about his watch. He came to a decision.

'All right,' he said. 'I *was* fibbing. I've got the key here. I was just thinking of what Mum would say, that's all. She wouldn't want – '

'She won't know,' Ginny snapped. 'Will she? Come *on*, Richard.'

He took the rusty key from his pocket and fitted it in the lock. Ginny, impatient, hopped from one foot to the other. Richard flung the door open. 'There you are,' he said. 'That's the cellar. I haven't got a torch so you can't see much.'

Ginny skipped inside, careless of the dark. 'Oooh, isn't it dirty?' she cried. 'Look at all the spiders' webs.' There was sufficient light filtering from outside to enable her to see a little of the interior.

'Don't go too far in,' Richard cautioned sharply, hurrying after her. 'You might hurt yourself.'

Ginny was oblivious. 'No, I won't,' she asserted. 'Try

and catch me!' She skipped ahead again, her shoes crunching over the floor.

'Ginny!' Richard called urgently. 'Don't be silly! It's pitch-dark in there.'

Virginia cupped her hands to her mouth and made a moaning noise. 'It's spooky,' she said. 'Oooh – oooh.'

Richard couldn't see her, she'd gone far ahead. Suddenly she shrieked. 'What is it?' he called, frightened.

Her voice sounded tremulous. 'There's – there's something in here,' she said. 'I think it's an animal. It rushed past me!'

Richard thought immediately of rats. 'Come back,' he ordered her sternly. 'You're being very naughty.'

A third voice, strange and distant, set the hairs on his scalp prickling. 'She's all right,' it said. 'It was only the cat.'

Richard's heart hammered painfully. 'Who – who is it?' he whispered. Ginny was silent. 'Ginny! Are you all right? Where are you?'

'She's here. With me,' said the strange voice.

Richard stumbled forward in the darkness, worried and scared. Suddenly the stranger struck a match and for a few seconds the cellar was illuminated by its flare. Richard saw a youngish-looking man, very scruffy in appearance, standing with his arm round Virginia and with his hand closed over her mouth. The girl looked terrified. Richard ran towards them. He recognized the man's dark unshaven face. Then the match died.

'Let her go!' Richard shouted. 'You've no right to do that. She's my sister and I'll fetch my parents.'

'No need for that,' said the stranger quietly. His voice was neither rough nor uncultured but Richard thought there was a kind of tenseness behind it. 'She'll come to no harm with me. And I'll let her go as long as you play the game my way.'

'What game?' Richard demanded. 'I don't know what you're talking about.'

'How did you get in here?'

'Through the door, of course.'

'Which door?'

'The cellar door. By the steps.'

'Oh.' The man sounded relieved. 'Right. Now, listen to me. You've got to promise never to come in here again, you and your sister. And to tell nobody about this place. Understand? Soon as you do, I'll release her.'

Richard wanted nothing else just then but for Ginny to be released and for them both to make their escape. He was quite ready to promise anything.

'I promise we won't,' he declared emphatically.

'All right. Off you go,' came the man's voice. Ginny, sobbing, hurled herself at her brother, flinging her arms around him. Richard responded, trying to comfort her.

'If you ever break your word, you're in trouble,' the man whispered menacingly. 'Do you understand me?'

'We understand,' said Richard. 'Come on, Ginny. Let's get out of here.'

The man lit another match. He wanted to be sure they were leaving. Richard, still holding Ginny to him, groped his way towards the daylight. He shut the cellar door behind him but, on impulse, didn't lock it. He thought it would be better if the man didn't know that he had a key.

The two of them were soon home. By then Ginny had calmed down a little. 'I wish we'd never gone there,' she said perversely. 'Horrid man! I think he was a tramp.' It never entered her head to wonder what he was doing there.

Richard didn't reprimand her for blackmailing him into taking her. He was really sorry she had had such a fright. But his brain was racing, trying to piece together the mystery of the strange man and the house. He realized the man was entering the house by the secret passage. But where was the entrance to that? And why was he going to the house? To steal old Mackie's valuables probably. It *must* have been this dark-faced man who had removed the china pieces that he and Ben had noticed were missing. And, Richard supposed, he must be selling them. Or was his main purpose to search for the Mackie hoard? Perhaps the antique pieces *were* the hoard. And what was this talk of a cat? What cat? Above all, where had this strange man come from? Richard was suddenly aware that Ginny had been saying something.

'Richard, *Richard*, you're not listening to me,' she accused him. 'Did you hear what I said?'

'No. I was thinking.'

'It's important. I was trying to tell you, that man was wearing your watch!'

— 5 —
The Boys Search the House

By agreement Richard and Ginny said nothing to their parents about the stranger who was also a thief – however, Richard, despite the man's warning, was determined to get his watch back. And that meant going back into the House of the Martins to confront the thief. He was furious that the man had simply taken it for his own, having found it where it had dropped. Richard knew it was only a matter of time before his father or mother commented on it.

Ben had hardly been able to wait until the next day to explore the passage and when Richard related to him the incident with Ginny, his eyes nearly popped out of his head. 'You saw him? He spoke to you?' he repeated each time Richard told him something new. 'He held Ginny? You had to promise? He was wearing your watch?'

'Yes, Ginny said he had it on,' Richard confirmed. 'But he's not going to keep it! And, as for the promise he made me give, that was only a promise not to go back with *her*. Well, I shan't. But *we're* not going to be stopped, are we?'

'Of course not,' said Ben resolutely. 'And him with your watch!'

They were soon once more in the cellar, shining their torches around and treading cautiously. Richard half expected to see a cat streak past them but they saw nothing moving. Then they came to the passage door. It was open. Ben shone his torch into the tunnel. It was not very wide, about three metres in diameter. It was brick-lined and the stony floor had been strewn with sand.

'It goes a long way,' he whispered. 'Look, it bends to the right – up there.'

Richard looked. They hesitated, then, without a word, went forward simultaneously. The passage felt cool and damp. They reached the bend and followed it round. The tunnel led on for perhaps another fifty metres, then came to a dead end. They saw a wall ahead of them with another door in it. After first listening hard and holding their breath, they tried the door. It opened into what seemed a square underground room. On another side of the room was a flight of steps leading up.

'I wonder where we are?' Ben whispered.

Richard had been doing some calculating. 'I think I know,' he answered. 'We're in that air-raid shelter in the neighbouring field.'

Ben glanced at his friend with admiration. 'Of course; I can see that now. Aren't you clever? The passage must have been built during the last War as a safe escape route from the house. And so this is where the man comes – '

'Hey! Look at this!' Richard interrupted him. He pointed to one corner. On a thick pile of newspapers there were some old faded pieces of material, neatly folded, and a sleeping-bag, much stained and crumpled. 'The man's been sleeping here,' he proclaimed. There were other items of use lying about – a portable camping stove, boxes of matches, a couple of saucepans, a kettle, a dish or two, some empty bottles of wine and a tin mug. A modest store of food in tins and jars was stacked against a wall.

'A squatter,' Ben summed up. 'He's made his home here.'

'Well, it's a base anyway,' Richard said. 'To be used while he hunts over the house. He must have discovered the passage by chance.'

'He must be planning to steal all the most valuable things bit by bit while there's still time,' Ben observed. 'But I wonder what's stopping him from doing a grand clear-out all at once and getting away?'

'Because he has to carry everything by hand,' Richard answered. 'He couldn't carry much at once. But I think he's here for another reason.'

Ben was agog. 'Do you? What?'

'I think he's systematically searching the place for the Mackie hoard.'

'Then you think there is such a thing. Really and truly, do you believe in it?'

'I'm beginning to,' Richard admitted.

'There's one way of finding out,' Ben said. 'By searching for it ourselves!'

'Yes, but Ben, if we found anything we couldn't keep it, you know. It wouldn't be ours, would it?'

'Of course not,' Ben agreed. 'What fun, though, to go on a treasure hunt! Especially when somebody else might be trying to get to the treasure first.'

His enthusiasm communicated itself to Richard who had been dubious about the scheme. He was mindful of the dark-faced man's threat. 'We'll have to go ever so carefully,' he said. 'I didn't like the look of that squatter man.'

'What could he do?' Ben blustered. 'He knows he's coming here illegally himself. And, anyway, you want your watch back.'

'I don't know if he could do anything or not,' Richard replied. 'But if he ever found out that we know he's stealing things . . .' He looked meaningfully at Ben who didn't fail to catch the warning.

Ben pursed his lips. 'Well, he's not around now,' he said, 'so let's make the most of it.'

'We'd better make sure first,' Richard counselled. He ran to the steps and leapt up them, two at a time. He had been correct. He found himself in the adjoining field, looking back towards the house. 'All clear,' he called as he ran back down. He and Ben hastened out of the shelter and back along the passage.

'Where shall we start?' Richard asked.

'Up in the house. The dining-room?' Ben hazarded. 'It doesn't really matter, does it?'

The boys didn't know what they were looking for. But they soon discovered one thing. A pair of silver candlesticks with which they had become familiar had now disappeared.

'There won't be anything left to auction soon at this rate,' Ben commented exaggeratedly.

'We ought to tell someone,' Richard asserted.

'Who?'

'I dunno. Our parents, I suppose. Then they could tell Mr Todd.'

'Trouble is,' said Ben, 'if we tell our parents now they'll know we've been getting in here and then they're bound to stop us. Why don't we see if we can find the hoard first?'

'All right.'

They went through the room methodically, opening cupboards, cabinets and drawers. Ben even looked under the rugs on the floor. Neither boy had a definite idea of what might be found but each boy's imagination conjured up visions of money or gold or jewels tucked away in some inaccessible place. They continued their search in the sitting-room and from there progressed to the other rooms on the ground floor. They found no treasure. Every so often they paused to listen for sounds of another intruder and one of them went periodically to the window to check the garden. But they were not interrupted. They proceeded to the study which was the last room to be searched on that floor. There was very little furniture in it. They looked in the desk. They didn't bother to scrutinise the shelves of books. There were so many volumes and they were so tightly packed together that they didn't imagine anything could have been hidden between them. They came to a halt. It was lunchtime.

'We can continue this afternoon,' said Ben. 'Upstairs. You never know – people sometimes stuff fortunes under their mattresses.'

'That's right,' said Richard. 'And I think there may be a real chance in old Mackie's case. You said your father complained that he didn't have a bank account.'

Ben rubbed his hands together. 'I can hardly wait,' he said. 'Let's not spend long over lunch. Tell you what, why don't you come over? We could have it together.'

'Yes, that'd be good. I'll just see my mum first but I know she won't mind.'

Mrs Bright raised no objections. She was going to be at home since it was early-closing in the shop and in any case she was pleased Richard and Ben were such firm friends.

Ginny knew about Ben's sister. 'Richard only wants to go so that he can see Angela,' she teased.

Richard coloured up and looked uncomfortable. 'Don't be silly,' he said awkwardly. He knew Ben was grinning at him. 'How would I know if she is going to be there?'

'She isn't actually,' Ben told him. 'She's playing in a tennis tournament with some other sixth-formers.'

Richard was disappointed and relieved at the same time. He thought Angela was terrific but he usually became tongue-tied in her presence.

Mrs Tompkins, a tall, elegant and somewhat serious lady, made the boys some tasty sandwiches and gave them ice cream. Richard was rather daunted by Ben's family and never thought Ben himself fitted into it properly: he was so unlike any of them. None of the others had coppery hair and freckles, nor did they have his happy-go-lucky personality.

Ben wriggled and squirmed on his seat all the way through lunch, he was so keen to get into the bedrooms of the House of the Martins. Richard, on the other hand, was on his best behaviour and Mrs Tompkins eventually remarked on the difference.

'You could learn a lesson in patience from Richard,' she told her son. 'Can't you just keep still for a second?'

'He's not often as quiet as this,' Ben declared. 'You should see him at school.'

'I can see him *now*. That's enough,' said Mrs Tompkins. 'He's a credit to his parents.'

Ben sighed and put on a prim goody-goody face for Richard's benefit. Richard was soon spluttering with laughter. Mrs Tompkins was obliged to smile. 'You're hopeless,' she said. 'Go on, the pair of you. Go and enjoy yourselves.'

'Thanks awfully, Mrs Tompkins,' Richard said politely.

Ben echoed this remark continually as they made their

way to the house. 'Thanks *awfully*, Mrs Tompkins,' he mimicked, accentuating the second word to a ridiculous degree. 'Thanks AWFULLY.'

'Oh shut up,' said Richard. 'You're an ace twit, Ben.'

'I wonder where the squatter's got to?' mused Ben as they climbed upstairs to the first floor of the house.

'He's probably flogging those candlesticks to a fence,' Richard answered. He was proud of his knowledge of a few words of criminal jargon.

Ben was already in the first bedroom. It had nothing in it except a very solid-looking walnut wardrobe which proved to be completely empty. Two other bedrooms had no furniture in them at all. The main bedroom, however, was where old Mackie had slept.

'Do you suppose he – um – died here?' Ben whispered.

'Probably,' said Richard.

They tiptoed about, almost feeling that the old man's presence was still in the room. They made a cursory search, not caring to meddle with any of the personal items Mr Mackie had only recently ceased to use. They were afraid to find his clothes still hanging in a cupboard or pressed in a drawer, vainly awaiting that re-usage that would never come.

'Shall we look under the mattress?' Richard queried softly. He and Ben exchanged glances. Ben pursed his lips. They both were loth to handle the thing which, stripped of its bedclothes, seemed to have a greater poignancy as the witness of old Mackie's last few breaths.

'It could be the very place,' Richard added.

'I s'pose we could just have a peep,' Ben answered.

The mattress was heavy. They lugged it up but had difficulty in holding it and suddenly they lost their grip and it thumped down again as if in protest at being disturbed. The boys scattered. They hadn't seen anything.

They had been into every room except the bathroom. They didn't feel like going in there and were going to pass it by when, through the open door, Ben spied something of interest on the windowsill. It was a book: a travelogue with a highly-coloured cover.

'That's funny,' he said.

'Not really,' Richard returned. 'Perhaps he read in the bath. My father does. He spends ages in there.'

'I didn't mean that,' Ben replied. 'I remember that book by its cover. Didn't we see it in the study this morning?'

'I dunno. Did we?'

'Yes, I'm sure we did. Look: *Fifty Years Of Travel* by Oliver Gumboe.'

'I can't remember,' said Richard. 'I didn't look at the titles much.'

'No, but don't you recognize the cover?'

'Sort of.' They looked at each other. 'Well, if it was downstairs this morning,' said Richard, 'you know what that means, don't you?'

'Let's go and check,' said Ben. 'See if there's a gap on the shelves.'

There was no gap. The selfsame book was where it had been in the morning, wedged between a guide to Venice and Lyle's *Antiques Review*. The boys were very curious. 'Why would he have two identical books?' Richard pondered.

Ben pulled the volume out and opened it up. 'Wow! Look at this, Rich.' The covers were false. It wasn't a book at all but a box and inside the box was a thick wad of very old, dirty and crumpled bank notes tied up with ribbon. The friends could scarcely believe their eyes. Ben lifted the notes out. There appeared to be hundreds of them and every one was worthless as currency. They were so old they had gone out of circulation decades ago.

'I don't believe this,' Richard muttered. 'We've found the Mackie hoard and it isn't worth anything.'

Ben's mouth gaped as he fingered the notes. A puzzled look came over his face. 'There's something hard inside them,' he said. 'I can feel it.'

Richard bent to look. 'Quick, take the ribbon off,' he urged.

Ben was in such haste that some of the notes dropped to the floor. They found that these notes were tied up separately in a smaller bundle. They were one-pound notes, the others were fives. In the middle of the wad of pound notes was a ring. It was a very old, thick gold ring, much worn, with a single blue stone set in the centre. Neither of the boys knew what the stone was. It wasn't like a gemstone. The ring was obviously ancient; the design was crude. Ben took out his handkerchief and tried to polish the thing a bit but he could make no improvement.

'Why keep it wrapped up with these?' he mused, riffling through the bank notes.

'For security, I suppose. The ring couldn't have been worn,' Richard pointed out. 'It's far too big for any finger.'

'What shall we do about it?' Ben asked. 'The money, I mean?'

'Nothing. It hasn't any value. But let's keep the ring for a while. I'd like to find out how old it is.'

All at once they froze. Footsteps could be heard below. There wasn't time to put the notes back in their hiding-place. Ben stuffed the pound notes in his pockets with the ring. Richard grabbed the five-pound notes, thinking to hide them behind a cushion. But as he cast around for a safe place the boys heard the trap-door being opened in the hall. Their first instinct was to run to a window. Richard was still clutching the money as the dark-faced man came into the room. Ben succeeded in getting a window open but the man's voice rang out, halting him.

'Stay where you are!' he shouted harshly. 'Or it'll be the worse for your friend!'

—6—
The Ring

Ben turned from the window. The man was staring at Richard. 'I thought you told me you wouldn't come here again,' he said to him. 'You're a nasty little liar, that's what you are.' Suddenly he noticed what was in Richard's hand. 'Hey! Come here, boy.' He cocked his finger and beckoned, a sly smile spreading across his face. 'I'll take that.'

Richard saw his watch, tied up messily with string, on the man's wrist and his fear evaporated. He was filled with righteous indignation. 'Give me my watch back,' he said coolly, almost imperiously.

'It's not yours,' the man growled. 'I found it.' But he seemed for a moment taken aback.

'Of course you found it,' Richard returned. 'I lost it in this house. You give me my watch and I'll give you this money.'

The man hesitated, apparently weighing up the possibilities of going for both. He relented. 'O.K.,' he said. 'You hand that money over now and I'll return the watch.'

Richard didn't trust him. 'Take the watch off first,' he insisted. Ben thought he was pushing his luck. 'Richard!' he hissed.

The man grinned. 'Huh!' he grunted. 'Your friend's

a bit more cautious. That's the way to deal with Donald Bone.' It was evident he was referring to himself. But he untied the watch nonetheless.

Richard stepped forward slowly. Bone stretched out his empty hand eagerly. Richard was watching the hand with the watch in it, assessing whether he dare make a grab for it. The exchange was made clumsily, the boy and the man determined to get what they wanted before relinquishing what they already had. Richard slipped his watch into his pocket with relief. Bone was counting the money. Richard and Ben smiled knowingly to each other. They thought the man was simple: that he didn't have the sense to realize he had a fistful of worthless paper. But Bone wasn't so stupid. He knew the old notes were marketable as collectors' items. There was money to be raised on them at a coin dealer's certainly.

'Come on, Richard,' said Ben quietly. There was no point in their remaining in the house any longer. The treasure hunt was over, Richard had his watch and, even more importantly, it was a good opportunity to get away from Bone while he was counting.

The boys ran out of the room and down into the cellar, switching on their torches. Bone shouted after them but they couldn't hear what he said and they ignored him. In the middle of the cellar, sitting placidly in their path, was a white cat.

'So there *is* a cat,' Richard whispered.

'Is it Bone's?'

'Must be.' Richard knew nothing about Mackie's pet. 'Perhaps it lives with him in the air-raid shelter.'

The cat unaccountably took an instant dislike to them, although they made no attempt to touch it. It arched its back and spat at them and, as Ben tried to sidestep the animal, it lashed out at him with extended claws in a sort of fury. Even through his jeans the boy felt the claws rake his leg. He yelled and ran for the far door. The cat disappeared into the darkness.

'What a horrible animal,' said Richard as they reached the garden.

Ben rubbed his leg. 'Whatever did it attack me for?' he asked ruefully. 'I *like* cats. Mimi's never done that to me.' Mimi was the Tompkins' pet.

'Of course not,' said Richard. 'She knows you and, anyway, that was no ordinary cat.'

'What do you mean?'

'It looked as if it was on guard. You know, as if it was protecting the place. Weird.'

'Well, I'm not going back in there,' Ben vowed as they cycled away. 'There's nothing more to look for anyway.'

Richard had a different opinion. 'How do you know?' he asked. 'There might be more loot stashed away behind those books.'

'I don't care if there is,' Ben answered. 'What good would it be to anybody? Mr Todd, the solicitor, ought to know about what we've found already and I think I shall tell my father everything tonight. Donald Bone is a criminal and should be arrested before he steals anything else.'

'We haven't any proof he is the thief,' Richard pointed out.

Ben stopped. He looked at Richard who came to a halt beside him. 'D'you mean you think we should just leave things?' he asked in disbelief.

'I'm not sure what to do,' Richard confessed. 'You see the trouble is, Ben, we may end up being suspected ourselves. If that Bone character is arrested he'll know who put the finger on him. What's to stop him saying he saw us stealing things?'

'Gosh, I hadn't thought of that.' Ben wrinkled his

brow. 'But surely, we can't let him carry on swiping things?'

'No. But I think I have another way of stopping him.'

'Go on, clever Dick.'

Richard laughed at Ben's unintended pun. 'We can stop Bone's entrance up. We have the cellar key so he can't get in *our* way. All we have to do is to pile up some heavy objects against the passage door and he's sunk.'

'Brilliant!' Ben cried, his eyes sparkling. Then his face changed. 'But that means going in again ourselves some time.'

'So what?' countered Richard. 'You're not getting scared, are you?'

'Not exactly,' said Ben. 'But there's a sort of atmosphere about that house, I can't explain it. I felt it all the time we were in there. As if we were being watched.'

'Didn't notice it,' said Richard. (This wasn't entirely true.) 'Anyway it only needs once more and then we're finished. And while we're in there we'll have a final look through the library.'

'You can,' said Ben. 'I'm not bothered any more. I'll help you block the passageway once we know Bone's nowhere about and that's it.'

Richard was a little puzzled. This didn't sound like the carefree, happy-go-lucky daredevil he was used to. Ben was renowned at school for his devil-may-care attitude. His high spirits and good humour were his most attractive features. And now he seemed unlike himself, as if his mood really had been influenced by the gloomy old house in some way.

'Where are we heading?' Ben asked.

'Wherever you like.'

'Shall we go back to my house? I can get rid of these notes and the ring then. Put them somewhere safe, because I don't want to carry them round with me.'

There it was again, that tone in Ben's voice, as if he wanted to free himself of anything to do with the House of the Martins.

Richard shrugged. 'O.K.,' he said.

Mrs Tompkins was gardening when they got to Ben's house. She greeted them briefly and went back to her weeding. Ben was glad to get the money and the strange ring out of his pockets and hidden without any questions being asked. He put the whole lot in his wardrobe inside an old pair of shoes.

'We'll ask someone about that ring,' said Richard. 'Would your dad be any help?'

'I don't know, but I'm not going to ask him.'

'Why not?'

'Because he'll want to know where I got it from, of course.'

'Say you found it somewhere.'

'That's hardly likely, is it? A ring of that sort you don't just find lying around in the street.'

'All right. We'll take it to a jeweller's some time.'

'Better still, how about the stamp and coin dealer's in the High Street? They have old medals and trinkets and things. They might know.'

'Good idea,' said Richard. Suddenly his ears pricked up. Angela had arrived home and was talking to her mother in the garden. He went as nonchalantly as he could to the window. Angela was still in her tennis gear. She was twisting stands of her long blonde hair between her fingers as she talked. Richard thought she looked stunning.

'I can hear Angela's voice,' said Ben, closing his wardrobe door. 'I wondered what you were so interested in.'

'No, I was only – '

'Come on, Richard, if you want to talk to her. She's always pleased to see you.'

Richard followed Ben half reluctantly out of the house and into the garden. Angela turned and gave Richard a wave and a broad smile. She liked Ben's friend who seemed so quiet and shy and completely unlike her brother.

'My, you've got a tan,' she complimented him as the boys came closer. 'Where did you get that?'

Richard smiled and blushed as he usually did. The blush gave his skin an even healthier glow. 'Nowhere really,' he answered softly. 'I s'pose it's just from being outdoors.'

'I wish I could tan that easily,' said Angela. 'Well, what pranks have you two been up to?'

'We've been digging for buried treasure,' said Ben with a grin, knowing full well he wouldn't be believed.

'Oh ha-ha,' said Angela sarcastically.

'Did you win?' Richard asked politely. 'I mean, the tennis?'

'Not the tournament, no.' Angela gave a silvery laugh. 'I'm not quite up to that.' She saw Richard felt foolish and rescued him. 'I did win a game or two, though. It was nice of you to ask me. I'd wait for ever for Ben to show any interest.'

Richard glowed.

Ben wasn't even listening. The Tompkins' garden fronted the Hallenden Road and he had just seen Donald Bone's head above the hedge. The man was walking fast. Ben ran over and peered through. Bone looked as if he was searching for something or someone: his head looked constantly from one side to the other. 'Richard! Richard!' Ben hissed.

'Excuse me,' Richard said to Ben's family and hastened to join his friend.

'Look through there,' Ben ordered, pointing to the gap he had made in the leaves.

'Bone!' Richard muttered. 'He's heading for the town.'

'I think he's looking for us.' Ben said. 'Look how he's searching about. I bet he's trying to track us.'

'Whatever for?' Richard wondered. Then he suddenly realized what an opportunity now presented itself to put their plan into practice. 'Hey, Ben!' he exclaimed. 'Now's the time to shut him out of old Mackie's house for good.'

Ben wasn't sure. If Bone *was* looking for them, he might come back. 'Isn't it a bit risky?'

'How can it be? We'll never have a better time,' Richard asserted. 'We actually know where he is. And he's going in completely the opposite direction.'

'At the moment, yes,' said Ben dubiously. 'All right then. Let's get it over with.'

They ran to their bikes. Richard's head was full of their plan and he was heedless even of Angela – well, almost. He just had sufficient grace to call 'goodbye' as the boys sped away.

'A sudden departure,' Angela commented to her mother with amusement.

'You know Ben,' Mrs Tompkins replied pragmatically.

The boys were soon at work in the Mackie cellar, piling up boxes against the passage door and reinforcing these by pushing the pieces of ancient furniture they had found earlier in front of the boxes. Anything that came to hand that had any useful weight at all was added. The friends stood back, panting, to survey their handiwork.

'D'you think it'll hold?' Ben asked.

'It had better,' Richard muttered grimly. 'Now, are you coming up to the study with me or not?'

'I – er – don't think I want to.'

'It'd be our last search,' Richard said persuasively.

'No. I'll wait by the cellar door. Don't be long,' Ben urged.

Richard went quickly up through the trap-door to the study and gasped at the sight that met his eyes. The room was in a shambles. There were books almost everywhere except where they were meant to be. The shelves were nearly empty. It seemed as if Bone had deliberately flung them all over the place – on to the furniture and particularly on to the floor – in a kind of frenzy. But why? As he stepped gingerly over the littered piles of volumes Richard's mind gradually worked out what must have happened. Bone had found him and Ben with the money and would soon have discovered the dummy travelogue that had contained it. The same thought had then occurred to the man as it had to Richard. Were there more of the same? And so in his greed and eagerness he had pulled out the entire collection of books in his search, hurling them about as he raided the shelves. There was no way of knowing if he had found anything else but Richard guessed he hadn't. What seemed more likely was that, as Ben and himself had got there first, the man would probably suspect they had made other discoveries and so was now in urgent search of them.

Richard's moral instinct told him he must put the room to rights. He simply didn't feel able to turn his back on the mayhem Bone had left behind him. Richard knew old Mackie must have treasured these books and, out of respect for the dead man's feelings, he began the labour of re-assembling the Mackie library. There were hundreds of books. There was no hope of putting them on the shelves in any sort of order but that didn't matter any more. Collecting half a dozen at a time, Richard commenced his task.

He soon realized that with Ben to help him the job

could be done in half the time. He went to the cellar steps and called for help.

'What on earth are you doing up there?' Ben called back. 'I thought we wanted to make a quick getaway. Have you found anything?'

'Yes,' Richard answered. 'Utter chaos.' He went on to explain.

Reluctantly Ben joined him under the stairs. 'Why do we have to pick the books up? We didn't put them there,' he complained.

'I just feel that we should, that's all. I'm surprised you don't.'

'Oh, all *right*, Richard. Don't go on.'

The room soon looked much tidier. Ben had ceased to collect up books and was kneeling in a corner, reading from a magazine that lay open on the floor. So automatic had Richard's movements become that it was a while before he noticed that Ben was no longer helping.

'Hey, Ben!' he cried eventually. 'That's not fair.'

Ben didn't respond at once. Then he slowly stood up, still holding the magazine and, with an air of suppressed excitement, said, 'Never mind the books. Come and see this!'

Richard joined him hastily. Ben's finger was pointing to a photograph in the magazine and it was trembling. It was a photo of the very ring they had found amongst the bank notes earlier that afternoon. Underneath the picture were the words 'The Manorbier ring: is it lost?'

'G-goodness,' Richard whispered.

There was a short article about the ring which the boys didn't stop to read just then. Their eyes, however, picked out words such as 'heirloom' and 'valuable antique' and this was enough to set their pulses racing.

'Where was this magazine?' Richard demanded.

'Just where I found it – over there.' Ben indicated the

spot on the floor. 'It was open at this page. More than a coincidence, don't you think?'

'Exactly. Bone must have seen it. *That's* why he's looking for us.'

'Oh, let's get away, Rich. Please. He'll be bound to return, even if he can't open the passage door. We left the cellar door open!'

'Crikey, so we did!' Richard glanced at the remainder of the books still lying about.

'We haven't got time for those,' Ben insisted. 'We've got to get away! Leave them!'

Richard was torn between the desire for flight and a nagging conscience. 'You go ahead. I'll finish up here and if you see anything give me a whistle.'

Ben scuttled away with the magazine. Richard raced about the study, gathering up the last volumes and stuffing them into the few spaces left on the shelves. Every minute he expected to hear Ben's whistle but nothing came. At last the job was done. Richard ran to the trap-door, down the steps and into the cellar. Ben was waiting for him nervously. As Richard came towards him Ben snapped, 'The cat! Behind you!'

Richard swung round. He saw nothing. He ran his torch over the cellar floor, then to the sides. There was no sign of the white cat. He hurried to the cellar door. The boys shut and locked it. 'The cat wasn't there,' Richard muttered. 'You must have imagined it.'

'How could I imagine it? It was there, behind you.'

Richard looked at his friend curiously. 'It wasn't, Ben. Honest.'

The boys were silent as they picked up their bikes. Both of them were glad to get away from the house. Richard was wondering again about its influence on Ben, and Ben was disturbed by the notion that he had been able to see something which Richard couldn't.

They looked cautiously along the road for any sign of the squatter before setting off.

'This magazine,' Ben said at last. 'It's very old, I looked at the date on the cover. February, 1952.'

'Did you read about the – er – ring?'

'N-no. I thought we could do it together.' There was a pause. 'Richard, I don't want to keep the thing.'

'We're not going to. We're going to get it valued.' Richard turned to his friend. 'Aren't we?'

'I don't care what it's worth,' Ben muttered. 'It doesn't belong to us – and – '

'And?'

'I think there's something sinister about it.'

—7—
Visions

In the seclusion of Ben's bedroom the two boys spread out the magazine on the floor. They lay full length on the carpet, their chins resting on their hands, feet kicked up behind them, and their eyes devouring the printed column under the heading: 'A Valuable Relic Gone Missing'. It was in a section of the magazine *Glorious Wales* called 'History and Legend'. What they had read about it made their eyes open wider and wider. The ring had belonged to the Machy family of Manorbier for generation after generation. The original owner had been a Welsh princeling, a giant of a man renowned for his strength as well as his size. He was known as Cawr y Cewri, Giant of Giants. The ring had been made for him to wear into battle against the Saxon English. There were various legends concerning it. One was that the Welsh prince had never lost a battle whilst his finger bore the ring. Thus it had become a good-luck token and so had been passed on through the generations. It was said to be fashioned from a Thracian gold cup. The blue stone in the centre of the ring was quite unlike any other mineral known to man. There were tales of it having fallen from the sky and present opinion was that it had once formed part of a meteorite. Through the centuries the ring had been lost, re-discovered, lost and found again. Somehow it had always returned to the Machy family. Legend had it that the ring had a strange power which worked adversely against anyone who was the wrongful owner, bringing him ill luck or suffering of some kind until such time as it was returned to the descendents of Cawr y Cewri. One thing was quite clear. The relic was immensely valuable. And, according to the magazine, in 1952 it had once again been lost.

'Fantastic!' Richard exclaimed. 'What a story.'

Ben wasn't so enthusiastic. 'I don't like it very much,' he said. 'It's eerie, all this stuff about bad luck.'

'I'm surprised you're not more interested,' Richard remarked. 'After all, you found the ring and so now it's as if we've become part of the legend.'

'That's what I don't like,' Ben declared. 'I've got the thing here in my bedroom. Supposing something happens?'

'Don't be daft. You don't *own* it, do you? It still belongs to Mr Mackie. We've just sort of – borrowed it.'

'Well, I just don't fancy keeping it here,' said Ben. 'When are we going to the numismatist's?'

'The what?'

'Numismatist. Coin dealer.'

'Show-off,' Richard grunted. He pulled out his watch. 'Too late for today. It'll have to be tomorrow.'

Ben looked unhappy. 'I really don't want that thing here overnight,' he said.

Richard misunderstood his friend's apprehension. 'Bone's not going to come to your house looking for it, is he?' he said dismissively. 'He doesn't know where you live.'

'I wasn't thinking of Bone,' said Ben in a low voice.

'What? You don't mean . . . you're not worried about this legend?' Richard was incredulous.

Ben didn't answer. He looked a bit sheepish.

'Oh, all right, give it to me,' Richard said with a superior air. 'I'll keep it till tomorrow.'

Ben leapt to his feet with alacrity and fetched the ring from the wardrobe. He left the old bank notes in his shoe. 'Here you are,' he said. He sounded relieved.

'Actually I think I ought to be going anyway,' Richard told him. 'We can meet early tomorrow and go straight away to the coin shop.'

'All right,' Ben agreed. He felt much brighter now. Then he said, 'I wonder where the ring was discovered last time? That magazine said it was lost in 1952.'

'Perhaps someone had stolen it and was forced to return it to the Machy family because of the curse of bad luck,' suggested Richard. He pronounced the name as if it were English, 'Maychee'.

'It's not "Maychee", it's Machy,' Ben scoffed. 'You know, the same as Mackie.'

'Oh.' Richard felt foolish. 'Yes, of course. Then why did Mr Mackie change his name – I mean the spelling?'

'Probably because he got fed up with people like you calling him "Maychee",' Ben chortled.

'Well, how was I to know? Anyway, the main thing is the ring did get back to the family.'

Ben was pensive. 'Who will it go to now?' he mused.

'No one.' Richard answered promptly. 'According to my dad old Mackie had no relatives. So it'll be sold along with everything else.'

The boys suddenly realized the significance of this situation. It would mean the ring would pass out of the Machys' keeping for ever! Would the ill fortune pass with it? The boys stared at each other. Both were dumb for a while, struck by the same thought.

'P-people should be warned,' Richard muttered. 'What if the ring does have this strange power?' He

examined the ancient heirloom anxiously as though he
expected it somehow to give him the answer.

'Who would warn them?' Ben asked shrewdly. 'Even
if Mr Todd or the auctioneers know of the legend – and
I bet they don't – they're not likely to put people off
buying anything. They're supposed to do the opposite.'

Richard nodded. 'Good point,' he said. 'We must
think about this, Ben. *We* know about the bad-luck business. Maybe we ought to do something?'

They came to no conclusions. Richard went home,
the ring in his pocket, still thinking hard.

During the night both the boys had what could only be
described as dreams. The ring and the money, the house
and old Mackie were so much on their minds that it was
not surprising that each boy's subconscious was deeply
affected. Their vivid imaginations, the games of make-
believe in the garden . . . all played a part. Yet to the
boys their night-time experiences seemed to them more
real than simple dreams.

Richard was convinced he was lying awake in bed
when in a kind of dim light at the foot of his bed he saw
a tall figure. It was a figure he recognized as being old
Mackie. The height, size and flowing grey hair made it,
to Richard, quite unmistakable. The figure didn't move
but just stood, looking directly at him, not exactly in an
accusing way but with an expression which could have
been interpreted as conveying the message: 'You know
why I'm here.' Richard sat bolt upright against the bed
headboard, rubbing his eyes. When he opened them
again there was nothing to be seen.

Ben had a similar experience though, in his case, he
was positive the figure had moved. Ben had never seen
old Mackie alive and so he only had Richard's description to go on. He awoke in the middle of the night with

a start. Someone was crossing his room, yet without making a sound. He saw it was a tall, big man with thick grey hair and the man was carrying a white cat. This figure turned and looked at him with a glance full of meaning. Ben was too frightened to speak so he pulled the bedclothes over his head. It was a long while before he dared emerge again. When he did the room was empty.

Neither of the boys mentioned these visions to their parents. They didn't think they would attract any sympathy, especially not from their fathers whom they thought might dismiss their descriptions as nonsense or nightmares. So they held their tongues until they had an opportunity to unburden themselves to each other. Ben began talking at once as soon as Richard was close enough. He was so excited and, at the same time, so unnerved that his flood of words was impossible to check. So Richard patiently heard him out and then said bluntly, 'Yes, that was Mr Mackie. The check suit you mention I actually saw him wearing when he was alive. And Ben, do you know what? He appeared to me too.' He went on to describe his vision.

This shared experience impressed Ben deeply. He began to jump up and down. 'He knows we've got it! He knows we've got it!' he kept chanting, referring to the Manorbier ring. 'We've got to give it back, Richard. Don't you see – he's haunting us?'

Richard waited for him to calm down. The importance of one facet of Ben's story had suddenly revealed itself. 'So the white cat obviously belonged to him, not Bone as we thought,' he mused. 'That must have been why it attacked you. It *was* guarding Mackie's hoard in his absence. It must have known *you had the ring!*'

Ben looked scared. 'Yes, yes, that's what it was. I

thought it was doing something like that at the time. Oh Richard, we must, must, MUST give it back.'

'But Ben, we can't give it back to old Mackie. You're not thinking clearly. He's dead. How can we give it back to him?'

'We'll just take it back to the house. That's all he wants. We can't do any more.'

'Then it'll be sold to somebody else, won't it?'

'I don't care, Richard, I don't care. That's nothing to do with us. I simply don't want us to keep it. We're both involved now, now that we've both had it in our keeping. We'll both suffer if we don't get rid of it.'

Richard pursed his lips. 'I don't want to keep it either,' he said. 'But I've been doing some thinking. We ought not to let it be sold, because I reckon old Mackie wanted to be buried with it. He knew he was the last of the Machy family.'

Ben gaped. 'But – but – why do you think that?'

'Well, don't you think that travel book we found in the bathroom was a bit of a coincidence? Why should it have been that very book that he left there? *I* think it was deliberate. He left it as a clue to the ring's whereabouts. And, although we didn't, I think we were meant to find that magazine at the same time. I'm sure it was tucked in amongst the books close to the false one, and left folded open at the page about the ring's history. He hoped the person who found them would put two and two together.'

Ben was impressed with these deductions, but he was still puzzled. 'Wouldn't it have been simpler for him to have worn the ring?' he suggested.

'You've seen the size of it,' said Richard. 'Old Mackie was big but the ring wouldn't have fitted him. That Welsh prince must have been a massive man.'

'Couldn't he just have had the ring about him some-where then – in his pocket or something?' Ben persisted.

'Even if he thought he was ailing he didn't know exactly when he was going to die, did he?' Richard pointed out. 'And he died in bed so that wouldn't have been any use. No, I really do think that book was a clue. And by leaving it in the bathroom it was more likely it would be taken notice of, than, say, by his bed as if he'd been reading it. People don't usually leave books around in a bathroom even if they read in the bath.'

'You *have* been doing some thinking, haven't you?' Ben murmured. Then he found another objection. 'Why didn't old Mackie leave an instruction about his ring in his Will?'

Richard shrugged. 'Perhaps he did. But you see, he must have known of the rumours about himself and his hoard. I bet he was afraid of being robbed. That ring has been stolen many times over the years. So he kept it as secret as possible.'

It all sounded quite plausible. Ben knew Richard was clever and so he was ready now to believe his friend's explanations. 'You'd make a brilliant sleuth,' he said admiringly.

Richard was pleased with himself. 'I just piece the evidence together, that's all,' he said pompously.

'Well, Sherlock, what do we do now?'

'Find where old Mackie was buried, of course.'

'What, you mean search the churchyard for his grave?' Ben was horrified but fascinated.

'What else?'

'You don't honestly intend us to start digging him up?'

'Don't be silly,' said Richard. 'We'd look like graverobbers. No, all we do is push the ring in some-where deep under a stone or the turf or something so

that no one will ever find it. That way he'll be as good
as united with it, won't he?'

'I think we should give the ring to Mr Todd to deal
with,' Ben said with conviction. 'I don't fancy this wandering around graveyards at night.'

'Who said anything about night?'

'Well, we'd be seen otherwise, wouldn't we?'

'Not if we're careful. And as for Mr Todd, can you
imagine him believing our story? No, we'd only get into
trouble for breaking into the house. We've been through
that before. We've simply got to do it ourselves, Ben.
It's as if Mr Mackie's depending on us.'

Ben shrugged. 'Oh well, if we must . . .'

'O.K. Let's go to the coin shop and see what they
make of it.'

The boys went slowly along Hallenden High Street on
foot. They wanted to appear as nonchalant as they could
in case Donald Bone was somewhere about, keeping his
eyes open for them. Secretly though, Richard felt as if
the Machy ring was burning a hole in his pocket.

The coin dealer, whose name Gordon J. Gossington
was inscribed over the doorway of the stamp and coin
shop, was busy with a customer so Richard and Ben
contented themselves awhile with looking in the window.
Coins, stamps, medals, tokens of all descriptions and
from a host of countries were arranged to tempt the
collector. Suddenly Ben tugged Richard's arm.

'Look at that!' he cried. 'He sells notes.'

'Where?'

Ben indicated the spot. Old bank notes – English,
American and European – were on sale and the boys
quickly noticed that the English ones were marked-up
above face value. Amongst these they recognized some

five-pound notes identical to the ones they had found and which Bone had commandeered.

'So this is where he brought them,' Richard muttered. 'If he sold all of them he would have made quite a bit of money. I never realized people collected old notes.'

Now the same thought entered the friends' minds but they saw that Gossington's customer was leaving the shop so they entered quickly before anyone else materialized. The bearded Gossington glanced up from his counter. He saw the two boys and guessed they had come to buy foreign stamps. 'Well now,' he said genially, 'what can I do for you?'

'Could you tell us what this is worth, please?' Richard blurted out, fumbling in his pocket. He handed the surprised coin dealer the ring.

'Good Heavens,' said Gossington, rather taken aback. 'This is a strange-looking item. Wherever did you get it?'

The boys thought quickly. Ben was first to answer. 'Er – it's a family heirloom,' he said truthfully.

'Is it now? And a very unusual one too,' said the dealer. He sounded intrigued. 'What an extraordinary stone. D'you know what it is?'

'It – it – came from another world,' said Ben. Richard pulled a face at him. 'I mean,' he enlarged, 'from a lump of rock from space.'

'A meteorite,' Richard summarized.

Gossington gave a wry grin. 'And who's been telling you tales like that?' he mocked them gently. Before they could say anything more he went on, 'I must admit, though, I've never seen anything like it before.' He scratched his head. 'The gold is very curiously wrought. It looks almost mediaeval to me. I'm afraid I can't begin to put a value on it. I've nothing to compare it with. I can only tell you it's very old. Very old indeed. That alone may be enough to make it valuable but you really need to see an expert if you want more information. A London dealer's, such as Sotheby's or Christie's might be the best people to try. Or the British Museum.' He turned the ring over and over. 'How long has it been in your family?' he enquired.

'Not very long actually,' Richard replied quickly. 'Thank you for your help.' He almost grabbed the ring back and ushered Ben to the door with the utmost haste. Gossington stared at them with astonishment as they left with such abruptness, his hand that had held the ring still raised in the air.

'What's the rush?' Ben complained. 'You were quite rude to that man.'

'I didn't mean to be but *that's* the reason,' Richard told him, turning him round so that he could see Bone striding down the High Street in their direction. 'I saw him through the window. Quick, let's run.'

'Where to?'

'Anywhere. Away. Then we'll double back to the churchyard when we've shaken him off.'

— 8 —
A Grave Discovery

Richard and Ben sprinted down a side road that brought them to the town's car park. Richard led the way. Here they paused to see if Bone was pursuing them. There was no sign of him.

'I don't think he saw us,' said Ben.

'Better safe than sorry. Come on, let's head down to the river bank, then along the footpath to Church Alley. We can approach the churchyard from the rear.'

They ran on. The river bank was deserted and so it was easy for them to see if Bone was following. He wasn't. They eased up and began to talk. Ben started chattering before his breath was back.

'Are you going to . . . do what the . . . man said about . . . taking the ring . . . to London?' he puffed.

Richard shook his head. When he could answer without gasping he said, 'It's not *that* important to know what it's worth. If we find where old Mackie's buried we can get shot of it now.'

'What about Bone?'

'He's nowhere about. I think he must have been on his way to the coin shop to sell more notes. It's obvious he didn't see us, so we're quite safe.'

'It's a pity in a way, though,' said Ben. 'I'd love to know about the ring's value.'

'Look,' said Richard patiently. 'Suppose we did keep it a bit longer. What would happen?'

Ben pondered. 'You're thinking of those visions we had?'

Richard nodded. 'They'd continue, wouldn't they?'

'I dunno. Perhaps we imagined them.'

'How could we both have imagined we saw old Mackie during the same night when we were in separate places? And your vision was different – he had the cat with him. Even before that, you thought you saw the cat behind me in the cellar. So that was a sort of vision too. That's when they started and they'll go on until we don't have the ring any more.'

'You can't be sure, Rich.'

'I'm not. But I don't want to risk it. You were more scared than I was, Ben. The thing is, we got so used to making up stories about that house: that it was haunted and so on, we haven't actually stopped to think what's happening to us. We've been visited by the supernatural! You read about these sort of things in stories but you never really believe in it all. And now we've actually experienced it ourselves.'

Ben blinked hard. Richard was right. They hadn't really thought about what was going on. 'We've got ourselves caught up in something unearthly,' he whispered, frightening himself as he said it. 'It's the power of the ring – we read that in the magazine. We're in its power, Richard. It's a power from another world and *it comes from that blue stone.*'

Now it was Richard's turn to take stock. The question of the ring's power and the source of that power hadn't occupied his mind very much. He felt that Ben's horrified words had uncannily identified the ring's secret. He gulped, swallowing hard. This adventure, which had begun with a bit of harmless exploring, threatened to get out of hand. He tried to pull himself together. But the knowledge that that strange ancestral ornament was even now in his pocket made him shiver visibly. 'We've got to remove it from our possession,' he said and was surprised to find his voice was shaking. It seemed as if the words had come unbidden to his lips.

Ben also was quaking. The friends looked at each other. Their fright at the situation they found themselves in was mirrored in each other's eyes. Instinctively they clutched at each other for comfort. Then, as if with one mind, they turned and ran into Church Alley.

Neither boy stopped until the churchyard was reached. They let themselves into it through the wicket-gate. The place was gloomy and, despite the sunshine, everything seemed to them to be shot through with a horrible foreboding. They began to search, first down one row of headstones, then moving along to the next. They passed quickly by any of those that were worn or overgrown. They sought only those that were newly inscribed. They silently scrutinized each of the new stones they found. Fortunately the churchyard was deserted, though in their present state of nerves the flight of a bird from a yew tree at the edge of the path made them jump.

They came to the last row of burial plots. None of the tombstones had the name Mackie on them. They turned to each other in bewilderment.

'Are there any more inside the church?' Ben wondered. 'Sometimes people are buried under the floor, aren't they?'

'Are they? Not these days, surely?'

'We'd better check it. You never know,' said Ben. Even as he said it he realized that, if they should find Mr Mackie's name carved on the floor of the church, there would be no way then in which they could return his ring to him. From the way Richard looked at him he knew he had come to the same conclusion. So they entered the church, fervently hoping not to make such a discovery.

They crept down the aisles, hardly able to draw proper breaths because their hearts were hammering so unmercifully. There was no new stonework, no new carving anywhere in the church. They were relieved but now they were faced with another problem. Where *was* the old man buried?

Ben shut the thick oaken church door behind them. They stood in the porch, irresolute.

'Now what do we do?' Ben queried.

Richard shrugged. 'Haven't a clue,' he said. 'There aren't any other churches in Hallenden. Can you think of anything?'

'I have thought of one thing,' Ben confessed miserably. 'The old boy may have been cremated.'

'Yes, I know. In which case we're sunk because Mr Mackie wouldn't exactly *be* anywhere then.'

Suddenly Ben brightened up. He struck his forehead as though he'd had a flash of inspiration. 'I've got it!' he cried. 'We can ask the Rector. He must have taken the funeral service. He'll be able to help.'

'Brilliant,' said Richard. 'The only thing is, wouldn't he find it odd, two boys asking about someone who isn't a relative?'

'Doesn't matter,' Ben returned. He was beginning to feel much more cheerful. 'We can say we want to put some flowers on his grave or something . . .'

'That's good,' said Richard. 'But who's going to do the talking?'

'I will,' Ben volunteered confidently. 'It's my idea.'

There was no difficulty in finding the rectory. Everyone in Hallenden knew where that was. They walked up

the gravel drive to the grand Victorian building. The
Rector's wife, Mrs Erskine, opened to their knock.

'My husband's in his study,' she told Ben in answer
to his enquiry. 'Is it important?'

Ben brazened it out. 'Well it is, rather,' he said.

'All right. Come in for a moment. I'll fetch him.' Mrs
Erskine held the door wide and the boys stepped into a
tiled hall. Presently the Rector came briskly towards
them with an expression that clearly illustrated his feelings at being interrupted.

'Yes. Yes, what is it?' he asked with resignation.

'It's about Mr Mackie from the House of the Martins,'
Ben said naively.

'Mackie? House of Martins?' the Rector repeated
blankly. 'I'm sorry, I don't understand.'

'Er – he died recently,' Ben said quickly. 'About two
weeks ago. There was a funeral and – and – we want to
know where he's buried,' he blurted out, completely
forgetting about the flowers.

'I don't recall any such name,' the Rector said. He
looked a little annoyed. 'If you can't make yourselves a
trifle clearer, I'm afraid I – '

Richard tried to explain. 'Mr Mackie. Who used to
have an antiques business. He lived on his own. An old
man on his own.'

The light dawned. 'Oh yes,' said Mr Erskine. 'I
remember now. There was a short Service of Remem-
brance in my church, but no funeral. The body was to
be taken for burial in Wales afterwards, I forget exactly
where. Why did you wish to know?'

The boys were dumbstruck at the news. They looked
at each other in distress. The Rector shifted impatiently
from one foot to the other. He didn't understand at all.
'What's the reason you want to know?' he repeated. He
could see they weren't at all happy at the news.

'We w-wanted to put some flowers on his grave,' Richard said in a small, barely audible voice.

'Ah. I see. I'm sorry. I'm afraid that's hardly possible in the circumstances. Well, if there's nothing else I can do for you . . . ?'

'No. No, thank you very much. We're sorry to have disturbed you,' Richard mumbled with his customary politeness.

The boys walked gloomily back down the drive. What had seemed like a simple solution had come to naught. They had reached a dead end. How *were* they to dispose of the ring? Neither Richard nor Ben had the answer.

'Wales!' Ben exclaimed. 'Why there?'

'The Land of his Fathers,' Richard explained. 'Remember the Welsh prince and the Machys.'

'I know all that,' said Ben. 'But old Mackie never lived in Wales, did he? I mean, if he ran a business in Kent . . . why would he want his body to be taken so far from his own home?'

'One very good reason,' Richard replied gravely. 'The ring. He wanted it returned with him to their homeland; to their hereditary home.'

'Manorbier,' whispered Ben, recalling the magazine article again.

'I think so.'

'Whereabouts is that?' Ben wondered.

'Don't know. Why don't we look it up in an atlas?'

They walked down Church Alley, this time in the other direction which led straight to the town. All thought of Donald Bone had gone from their heads. Back in the High Street they suddenly came face to face with him. He looked a little less grubby and shabby than when he had confronted them in the Mackie house. He was clean-shaven which made his sallow complexion look sort of yellowish.

'I've been looking for you two,' he said without preamble.

'What for?' Richard asked sullenly, though he knew quite well.

'You've got something of mine, I think,' said Bone.

'Oh no, we haven't,' Ben said. 'What could we have of yours?'

'It's — er — something I mislaid,' Bone went on. 'In that house where we talked before. I can't find it anywhere. I must have dropped it in that room — you know where I mean. And now I can't go back to look for it, thanks to some *clever* individuals.' He began to sound menacing.

'We've got nothing of yours and we don't want anything to do with you,' Richard told him. He knew what Bone was angling for. He went to walk on. Bone barred his path.

'I think you'd better hand it over before you regret it,' said the man.

'Get lost,' Richard cried and ran. Ben pelted after him. They ran automatically for the House of the Martins. Richard could think only of returning the ring to its hiding-place. He didn't want it in his pocket, nor in his own house. He was afraid of more visions. But, when they got there, they saw to their dismay that the house had suddenly become the centre of activity. Mr Todd the solicitor could be seen in the hall conversing with two other men in smart sober suits.

'Oh no!' wailed Richard. 'Now we're really stuck with it.' He was beginning to feel as though the old ring was their evil charm.

'I wonder what's happening?' said Ben as they came to a halt outside the house. 'I s'pose it's something to do with the auction.'

'Whatever it is, we can't put the ring back. We'll have to hide it somewhere. I'm not taking it indoors again.'

'Nor me,' Ben concurred. 'But it'll need to be somewhere safe from Donald Bone. It's obvious he knows we've got it.'

'Let's bury it,' said Richard. 'In Mackie's garden.'

'We can't go – '

'No. No, later. When they've all gone.'

It wasn't until the afternoon that the coast was clear. Richard and Ben, armed with a trowel, dug a small hole by the dilapidated garden shed in which they had found the cellar key. They covered the ring over with earth and flattened it down. Then they spread some dead twigs and leaves and stones over the spot. They were confident that no one could discover the place. And they were consoled by the fact that Bone's visits to the house had now been curtailed permanently.

When they had finished with the ring they decided to dispose of the cellar key as well. Richard locked the cellar door and went to return the key to the selfsame hook inside the shed. As he opened the shed the white cat appeared as if from nowhere, howled at him and streaked off down the garden towards the neighbouring field, disappearing into the air-raid shelter. He was relieved to find that Ben had seen it too.

'Thank Heavens, it wasn't another vision *then*,' he muttered with relief.

'No,' said Ben. 'That was real all right. It must be living wild,' he went on, 'since its owner died.'

'I think Bone's looking after it,' Richard returned. 'Did you see where it went?'

'Into his squat,' said Ben distastefully. 'He'll have to be clearing out of that now. And *we'd* better be off too. Those men could come back at any time.'

'Well, good riddance to that,' Richard said with feeling, glancing at the patch of debris under which the ring was hidden. 'I say,' he remarked. 'We really did quite a good job, didn't we? It's very well concealed.'

'Not bad,' Ben agreed. 'Now let's go and look that name up in my atlas. I've got a good one with large scale maps.'

Manorbier turned out to be a very small town in the south-west of Wales, in the county of Dyfed. It looked like a remote sort of place to the boys.

'Well,' said Richard, 'that must be where Mr Mackie went. If so, he's a long way now from the Machy ring.'

'What does it matter,' said Ben carelessly, 'he'll never know anything about it.' As soon as the words were out of his mouth he realized his foolishness. He clamped a hand over his lips as if mentally he was forcing them back. He really felt he had tempted Fate. He looked very distressed.

Richard's dark brown eyes, too, had a look of alarm in them. The boys stared at each other, not daring to voice their thoughts. Ben put the atlas away but they couldn't put their ideas behind them.

'Of course we d-don't know for sure where he went,' Ben said in a small voice.

'No. That's true,' Richard answered. But neither of them could take comfort from that.

'Let's go and kick a ball around; put it out of our minds,' Ben said with bravado. 'I'm sick of the whole thing. I want to think about something else.'

But they couldn't think about anything else. Listlessly they kicked a football around the Tompkins' garden, hardly speaking to each other. Each was afraid of what the other might say. Finally they became so downcast they decided to part for the remainder of the day. Both boys felt a need to be amongst the rest of the family.

Both sets of parents and sisters, too, were quick to notice the boys' gloominess which, in holiday time, was very unusual. Ben in particular was normally such a live wire that his lack of spirits was all the more remarkable. Mr and Mrs Tompkins asked him if he was feeling unwell. Ben mumbled a denial but threw no light on the cause of his mood. They didn't question him further. Angela was of the opinion that he and Richard had had an argument and fallen out, something that happened occasionally. As for the Brights, they were unable to get a word out of their son. Richard could be taciturn at times.

'He's sulking,' piped up little Virginia. 'I bet Ben beat him at cricket!'

— 9 —
Mr Mackie's Will

The truth was, both Ben and Richard were dreading going to bed. They were convinced that something would happen during the night and they didn't know how to prevent it. Richard felt the only course open to him was to try to ward it off as long as possible by remaining awake. However the excitement and the anxiety of the day had worn him out and he was asleep by midnight. It wasn't many minutes before he started to dream. His mind was full of ghosts and ancient warriors, Cawr y Cewri and Donald Bone.

He first dreamt he was being chased by Bone along a deserted street. It wasn't clear in the dream why he was being chased and this rather vague set of images gave way abruptly to much sharper ones. This time the scruffy burglar wasn't in evidence. Richard saw Ben standing a long way off, on top of a mound, beckoning to him. Richard tried to reach him but his legs wouldn't carry him along properly. Someone was tugging him back and, when he turned to see who it was, he found himself staring into the face of Mr Mackie. It wasn't an unpleasant face but old Mackie looked very determined and, in a way, almost desperate to pull Richard away in the opposite direction. Richard soon found he was being propelled towards a railway station. In front of the station a number of people seemed to be waiting for him. They were strange people. He didn't know who they were and some of them were wearing old-fashioned clothes from different periods of the past. Mackie was trying to push Richard amongst them. Richard was very frightened and cried out. Then he woke up with a tremendous start.

It was a few moments before he realized he was awake. His heart was hammering and some of the dream must have carried over into reality because he had a sense of not being alone. He reached out for his bedside lamp and flicked it on. The room, thankfully, looked as it always did. Richard tried to calm himself. Suddenly the door opened. It was his mother.

'Are you all right, dear?' she asked solicitously. 'I heard you call out.'

Richard rubbed his eyes. 'Did I?' he muttered, remembering the details of the dream.

'Have you had a nightmare?' asked Mrs Bright.

'I – er – well, sort of,' Richard told her.

'Oh dear, how nasty. Never mind, it's all over now. Try not to think about it.'

Richard was doing just that. His mother's presence was very comforting. He looked at his watch. It was only twelve-thirty but it seemed to him as if he had been in bed for ages. His mother followed his glance. 'Oh, that needs a new strap,' she said. 'Why didn't you ask Daddy?'

'I – I forgot.'

'Oh well, I'll tell him, don't worry. Now, can I get you anything? A drink or something?'

'Thanks, Mum. That would be nice.' Richard realized all at once he was sitting bolt upright. He settled back under the bedclothes.

'Won't be long,' said his mother and tripped out

again. Richard heard her running downstairs. She always ran up and down very quickly and there was something so reassuring in the sound that he began consciously to relax. Then, before his mother returned, his thoughts strayed to Ben. He couldn't help wondering if Ben might suffer a similar incidence.

Ben had. He had gone to bed in trepidation. Somehow Mackie's white cat had got on his mind, probably because of what had happened before. He was afraid of seeing its ghostly shape prowling about his bedroom at night and so, of course, when he fell asleep, this was exactly what he did see. The animal jumped on to his bed and sat watching him malevolently. At any rate that's how it seemed to Ben. It wasn't a large animal, yet it apparently had a tremendous weight. It pressed down on the covers relentlessly so that Ben felt he was pinned underneath. He began to feel stifled and struggled against it. But the more he struggled, the more the weight pressed down. Ben was sinking and sinking down . . . Abruptly the pressure ceased. The cat vanished and Ben found that, instead of lying beneath the bedclothes, he was actually covered by hundreds and hundreds of bank notes to a depth of half a metre. Every one of the bank notes had the one word printed on it: Manorbier.

Ben was awakened by a persistent cry. It was a harsh unvarying miaow coming from the garden. He got out of bed. The white cat was sitting on the lawn. As soon as Ben looked out the sounds ceased. The cat looked up at him. Ben wasn't sure if he had been dreaming or not. He stared at the cat. Eventually it moved away. Ben didn't go back to bed for a long time. He kept thinking of the bank notes. Manorbier. Then he thought of Richard and he knew, as sure as though his friend were standing next to him, that Richard was thinking of him, and that the same thoughts were passing through his mind as were passing through his own. *That they had to take the Machy ring back to Wales*. They had to find its rightful place because only then would these visions stop.

The next morning Ben wasted no time before contacting Richard. Immediately after breakfast he went to the phone and dialled the Brights' number. It was a Saturday and so, in both houses, the entire family was around. Ben knew he must be careful what he said. However the situation was made very much easier by Richard who answered the call and said, 'I knew you were going to phone.'

'I thought you might,' said Ben. 'Did you have them?' he asked cryptically, meaning the visions.

Richard knew what he meant. 'Yes,' he answered. 'Did you?'

'Yes. You know what we've got to do?'

'Yes. When shall we meet? We've got to make our plans.'

'It's a bit difficult,' Ben said. 'We're all going out, I think for lunch. So I'm not sure when we'll be back.'

'Right. Ring me when you get home,' said Richard. 'I'll be here with Ginny. Mum and Dad are going to the shop this morning. I think Mum's coming home at midday.'

They rang off. To their parents, both boys again seemed subdued. This was because their minds were pre-occupied with the preparations they would need to make. The boys were apprehensive, yet excited by the prospect of a real adventure. The thing that bothered them more than anything else was how they would go about locating the place where old Mackie's body had been taken. Richard did have a brainwave. The Brights knew Mrs Crisp, Mackie's housekeeper, vaguely. Richard had a feeling she would be the person to ask about Wales because she had had closer contact with the old man than anyone.

It was late afternoon when Ben phoned again. He said his parents had told him he could go out for a couple of hours before supper-time. Richard invited him round. When he arrived the boys went into the Brights' garden. They described their dreams to each other. Then Richard told Ben about his idea concerning Mrs Crisp.

'Where does she live?' asked Ben.

'Only a few houses down the road,' Richard replied. 'Shall we go now?'

'Yes, but we're going to have the same problem that we did with the Rector. She'll want to know why we're asking.'

'I know and I can't think of any excuse at all,' Richard admitted.

'Why don't we just come straight out with it then?' Ben suggested.

'She'll be suspicious.'

'Of course, but does it matter as long as we get the information we want?'

'Dunno,' said Richard. 'I tell you what, we could pretend we're calling on her to tell her about the cat. And then work our way round to the other business.'

The cat was a sore point with Ben. His eager face clouded over. 'Tell her what about the cat?' he muttered, kicking the ground with the toe of one shoe. 'Ghastly creature.'

'Well, that – that someone needs to look after it,' Richard hazarded. 'It was Mackie's pet, wasn't it? I don't expect Bone is caring for it properly. He doesn't even look after himself.'

Ben looked at Richard askance. '*Is* there really a cat?' he murmured.

Mrs Crisp opened her front door. Her face registered surprise. 'I don't need any jobs done at the moment,' she warned them, thinking they were bob-a-jobbers.

'No,' said Richard, 'we're not Scouts, Mrs Crisp, we've seen Mr Mackie's cat.' Ben hung back.

'Cat?' she repeated. 'Nonsense. It disappeared the day he died. I'm sure it must be dead too.'

Ben backed away.

'A white cat,' Richard insisted. 'In Mr Mackie's garden. Perhaps it's looking for him,' he added cleverly.

'Well, it won't find him then,' she answered. 'He's gone for ever, poor man. He's not even buried round here, but down in Wales. No, it must be another cat.'

Richard forgot about the cat. 'Wales?' He pretended astonishment. 'Why Wales?'

'He wanted to be buried there.'

'Whereabouts?'

'Oh, a little village somewhere. Now whatever was it called?'

'Manorbier?' Ben suggested.

'Yes, that's right. That was it. How ever did you know?' She looked more than puzzled. 'Now what is all this?'

'Nothing,' said Richard. 'We were – um – worried about the cat.'

'Well, I can't do anything,' Mrs Crisp said. 'My duties are over in respect of that house. I can't look after any cat. My husband's not well and we've got goldfish in any case.'

It sounded so ridiculous Richard started to giggle and pretty soon Ben joined in.

Mrs Crisp was cross. 'Wasting my time,' she com-

plained. 'You boys are all alike. Haven't you got anything better to do? I'll tell your mother, Richard Bright.'

'Sorry,' Richard spluttered. 'We didn't mean to – ' He
tried to stifle his laughter. Mrs Crisp slammed the door.
The boys' merriment soon came to an end.

They walked solemnly away. At last Ben muttered,
'How do we get to Manorbier?'

'By train, I suppose,' said Richard. Neither of the boys
knew very much about trains. They travelled almost
everywhere by car. They looked thoughtful.

'I know how to get to London,' said Ben helpfully.

'Yes. So do I,' said Richard. 'But Wales? I haven't a
clue. I've never been there.'

'Well, we can't ask our parents,' Ben said emphatically. 'They'd soon get the story out of us and that would
be the end of everything.'

'Except the visions,' Richard commented. 'Oh Ben,
how are we to get out of all this? I'm really scared. I
don't know what's happening to us. And how are we to
travel all that way without our parents' knowledge?'

Ben, appealed to in this way, felt a sense of responsi-
bility. He was a few months older than Richard and he
suddenly felt grown up. He pondered his new status.
Then he looked at his friend. 'Subterfuge,' he answered
succinctly.

'What?'

'We'll leave a false trail.' He came to a stop. They
were nearing Richard's house. Ben lowered his voice to
a secretive whisper. 'Look, tomorrow's Sunday. So we
can't do anything then. But I can ask Angela to help.
She'll know about trains. I'll make sure she doesn't
suspect anything. Then tomorrow night we must pack
some clothes and things. Have you got a bag? Good.
Keep everything well hidden and only put in what's
absolutely necessary and what won't be missed. Then

we'll write notes explaining what we're doing without giving any of the details. All right so far?' Richard nodded dumbly. 'O.K. Then, on Monday morning, we leave the notes somewhere where they won't be discovered immediately. We smuggle our bags out somehow, we take our bikes and tell everyone we're going out for a ride – you know, just as if we're going into Hallenden. Only we go to the station. We get the train to London and then' – he waved his arms – 'off we go to Wales.'

'When shall we fetch the ring?'

'Monday morning. Before we set off. We don't want it indoors, do we?'

'No chance,' Richard answered vehemently. 'But Ben, just think, we've got two nights to get through before we can even start. I'm really afraid of the night-time now.'

Ben had got so caught up with his plans he had temporarily forgotten about this aspect. 'Perhaps we won't be bothered so much now we've decided to do something positive,' he said without a lot of conviction. 'You know, if he realizes we're trying to help.'

'He? You mean old Mackie?'

'Yes.'

'How can he know?' Richard demanded with a hint of anger. 'He's dead, Ben! We're beginning to believe all of this silly legend business.'

'I believe it,' Ben admitted, almost inaudibly. 'I really do, Richard. And so do you, don't you? Otherwise why are we making all these plans?'

Richard's face revealed all. He nodded. 'What do we do about train times?'

'Dad's got a train timetable for trains to London. We'll have to find out the rest when we get there. But

Angela will work out a route. She won't know why she's doing it – I'll think of something.'

'We'll need money,' Richard pointed out. 'I haven't got much. What about you?'

'I've got some saved up for when we go on holiday,' Ben answered. 'I don't know if it'll be enough, though.'

'We'll have to buy food and things,' said Richard.

'Yes. Richard, I've just thought!' Ben cried, forgetting all at once about the need for caution as he had another of his flashes of inspiration. 'The notes! That's why I dreamt about being covered in notes!'

'What *are* you on about?'

'Those old bank notes in my wardrobe,' Ben said impatiently. 'We can sell them, just like Donald Bone did. At the numismatist's.'

'Ben, you're brill! What's the time?' Richard's father had taken his watch to have a new strap fitted. Ben told him. 'Right, we've still got a little time left. The shop probably hasn't closed yet. Let's go now!'

The boys ran for all they were worth, picked up their bikes from the Brights' front garden, and cycled madly away. Mrs Bright and Virginia saw them go. Richard's mother shook her head. 'Why always in such a hurry?' she murmured.

'It's only high spirits, Mummy,' Virginia said precociously, remembering her mother's words.

Gordon Gossington was just closing shop when the boys arrived, panting from their exertions, in his doorway. He recognized them from their previous visit.

'I'm sorry, lads, you're too late this time,' he told them. 'I'm closed till Monday.'

'Oh, Mr Gossington, please, couldn't you just spare us five minutes?' begged Ben. 'That's all it would take.'

'If it's another valuation you want, I'm afraid not,' said the coin dealer.

'It isn't,' Ben answered. 'We've got something to sell.'

Gossington raised his eyebrows. 'Really? Have you found another heirloom perhaps?'

'No, it's this.' Ben pulled the notes from his pocket in a lump and thrust them at the man.

Gossington frowned. 'This is odd,' he muttered. 'There seems to be a glut of these around Hallenden at the moment.' He motioned to the friends. 'You'd better come in.' Inside the shop he looked at them curiously. 'Where did you get these?' he asked.

'We f-found them,' Richard replied too hastily.

Gossington's eyes didn't move from their faces. It was obvious he didn't believe them. 'Are you sure you haven't been having dealings with a certain scruffy, swarthy individual who's recently appeared on the scene?'

The boys knew he was referring to Bone. 'No!' they both said simultaneously, indignation written plain on both faces.

'All right,' said Gossington reluctantly. He counted through the old notes. 'They're not worth an awful lot,' he told them. 'I can give you twenty pounds and no more. I've really too many of these already. But you can take it or leave it, I'm not bothered.'

The boys exchanged looks. They had no idea what the notes were worth. They nodded at each other. 'We'll take it, please,' said Ben.

Gossington went to unlock his till. 'There's one condition,' he added. 'And that is that you tell me where you found these notes.'

Ben and Richard were embarrassed. They hadn't rehearsed an answer to such a question. Gossington was taking four five-pound notes from the till. He held them in his hand. 'Well?' he prompted.

'Well, they – er – they were in an old wardrobe actually,' Ben managed to extemporize.

'A wardrobe. I see. Where?'

'At home.'

'Oh. In your own home? Hm. All right. I'm not sure I can *quite* picture it but – very well, here's your money. And please, boys, don't bring me any more.'

'There isn't any more,' Ben said truthfully, taking the twenty pounds. 'Thank you, Mr Gossington. Goodbye.'

Ben and Richard left the shop, almost delirious with their success. Twenty pounds!

'And it's not as if it's theft,' said Richard. 'Because we'll spend it on doing Mr Mackie's will.'

—10—
An Omen?

Taking all the money they had into account Richard and Ben were able to muster fifty-seven pounds and eighty-one pence between them. They spoke together on the phone on Sunday after Ben had tackled Angela. He had tried to make his question about travelling to Wales a theoretical one, first ensuring his parents were out of the way in the garden.

'Ange, supposing you suddenly had to take a train to Wales, where would you go from?'

'Wales? Well, London, of course.'

'I know, but what station?'

'Not sure, Ben. Wait a minute – Wales is westward – probably Paddington.'

'Oh. And where would you get off?'

'What a daft question. You'd get off where you had booked your ticket to, obviously.' Ben's beautiful sister was experimenting with a new make-up and was seated in front of a mirror examining herself. She was a little vain but she had reason to be.

'Oh, Ange! Don't be awkward,' said her young brother. 'Look, if I show you a place on a map can you tell me how I'd get there? You see, we have problems like this in Geography sometimes and I've never been too good at working them out.'

'All right, give me the data. I'll show you how,' Angela offered, generously enough.

Ben promptly pointed to Manorbier on his atlas which he had, of course, already opened at the correct page. Angela pushed back her blonde hair and peered at the dot in the Dyfed countryside.

'That's a remote village – that doesn't count,' she told Ben. 'There wouldn't be a station there.'

'But where's the nearest one? You'd have to go to *that*, wouldn't you? You know, to reach Manorbier.'

'Oh, this is suddenly so important to you?' Angela cried irritably. 'Can't you see I'm busy?'

'Yes – beautifying yourself as usual,' Ben quipped with a grin. 'You did promise to help, though.'

'O.K. I'll do it.' Ben's sister held up her hands to avoid further badgering. 'Let me finish here and I'll jolly well find out how to get to Timbuktu if you want.'

Ben was satisfied. He left Angela alone. Eventually she emerged from her bedroom, went to the telephone and contacted British Rail. She returned with an exact run-down of all the relevant information which she read to Ben in an utterly toneless voice as if she were a slave robot. 'Paddington to Swansea. Change trains. Take train to Tenby, nearest station to Manorbier. Trains leave Paddington on the hour.'

Ben tittered and took the piece of paper from her. 'Thanks ever so much, Ange. Aren't I lucky to have a machine who obeys my every command?'

Richard was duly apprised of the route in a whisper. The boys were bubbling with an excitement which was overlaid by a sense of relief. They had very soon established from each other that neither of them had had a visitation the previous night. They had both been so tired after their previous interrupted nights that they seemed to have enjoyed dreamless sleep. Richard agreed to phone Ben that evening when he had made all his arrangements. The message was to be: 'Everything's in order here.' Ben was to reply: 'Check.' He thought that was the most professional response. Then, on the Monday morning, they were to meet by the old shed in the garden of the House of the Martins, having left cryptic notes behind them for their parents to find later in the day. They were to bring money, bags, bikes and any food they could safely pilfer, along with them. Then it was just a question of unearthing the ring and scooting off to Hallenden Station. They thought their arrangements were quite perfect. Unfortunately they had made no allowances for possible snags.

Richard began packing his old clothes in his sports bag in the afternoon. Every now and then he paused to admire his brand new watch-strap. He remembered to pack a comb, his toothbrush and a towel and then he went to the bathroom cupboard and took out a spare tablet of soap and a tube of toothpaste. He couldn't think of anything else he needed except his money which was already in his pocket. Then he suddenly remembered pyjamas and that made him stop and think. Where on earth would they sleep? He shrugged. Perhaps they could go to Wales and back in one day. At that stage he didn't understand much about the time and distance that would be involved. While he was busy his parents and Ginny were in the garden enjoying the sunshine. Richard cast about for things in his room that he might need. He added his torch and a notebook and pen to his packing. Then he ran downstairs to the kitchen. The rest of the family was still heedless of his preparations. He took a packet of biscuits, some cheese, a tin of baked beans and a tin of hot-dog sausages from the cupboards. Then he got a couple of cans of Coke and a carton of juice. He didn't think of including a tin-opener. He rushed back upstairs, stuffed the provisions into his bag and pushed the bag under his bed. Then he sat down on the bed to compose his message to his parents. It wasn't easy.

He suddenly felt terribly guilty and unhappy. He knew how worried his mother and father would be by his disappearance. He felt he'd rather do anything than upset them. For a few fraught moments he wrestled with his conscience, almost bringing himself to the point of deciding not to go. After all, if the dreams or whatever they were had stopped . . . But how could he let Ben down? And then in his mind's eye he saw Mr Mackie, angry, threatening . . . and quietly he began to write:

Dear Mum and Dad, I've got to go somewhere with Ben. I can't tell you exactly where because you would come after us. **DON'T WORRY**. *I'll be back very soon and will tell you everything. It won't take us long and we have to do it because no one else can. I hope you understand. We have got some money with us. Love, Richard.*

He was still looking at his scrawl, wondering if he should add anything else, when Virginia walked into his room. Richard quickly pushed the note in his pocket.

'What are you doing?' asked Ginny. 'Mummy and Daddy sent me to find you.'

'I'm not doing anything,' said Richard gruffly.

'You were writing something – I saw you.'

'It's nothing. Just a game.'

Ginny looked at him curiously. 'Are you still going into that old house?' she asked.

'No.'

'I think you are. I bet you and Ben are up to some-thing.'

Richard pretended to be cross. 'Don't be silly, Ginny. And mind your own business.'

'It *is* my business. We were warned by that man not to go there again. So there.'

'I tell you I'm not any more. Didn't you hear me?'

Ginny looked tearful. 'Oh Richard, please, please don't play there,' she wailed. 'I'm afraid of that place. There's something horrible about it. I don't want you to get hurt.'

Richard softened at this unaccustomed display of concern on his little sister's part. He knew she loved him really, just as he did her, despite their childish squabbling. He got up and put his arms round her.

'Don't worry about me,' he said. 'I can look after myself. Hey, come on, Ginny, what's the matter? I didn't mean to upset you.'

'You h-haven't,' she sobbed, clinging on to him. 'But I've had a horrid dream about you and it – it – frightened me.'

Richard paled. 'A dream?' he whispered. 'What sort of a dream?'

'You were in danger,' she wept. 'A long way away and – and – we couldn't get to you.'

Richard was shocked. He trembled slightly. Surely Ginny wasn't having the visions as well? 'Look,' he said hastily. 'I'm here, aren't I? I'm not a long way away.' He felt like a liar as he said it. 'Come on now. Let's go and play a game and forget all about it. Tell you what – you can choose whatever game you like.'

Ginny appeared to brighten up. Richard wasn't often so magnanimous towards her. 'Can I?' she chirped. 'Oooh – good.' She tugged him from the room, then downstairs and towards the garden.

Early the next morning, after breakfast, Richard looked

around for a good place to leave his note. He wanted it to be noticed, but not at once. He needed enough time to be well clear of Hallenden and, he hoped, London too, before it would be found. He had put it in an envelope which he had addressed very formally to 'Mr and Mrs G. Bright'. He decided not to leave it downstairs where someone might come across it too soon. So, having made his bed, he simply tucked one corner of the envelope under his pillow, leaving most of it exposed to anyone's gaze who might look in. He thought his mother was the most likely person to find it. His father would be at the shop all day and Ginny hardly ever had cause to go into her brother's room.

Richard was feeling refreshed from another uninterrupted night's sleep and he was eager to get going. The phone message to Ben the previous evening had worked perfectly well and now Richard had a stroke of luck. His mother had to take Ginny to the dentist.

'Now, Richard, we won't be long,' said Mrs Bright, 'but if you want to go out, for goodness' sake make sure all the windows are closed first. And take your key with you.' This was unnecessary advice since Richard was very careful and methodical with such things.

Mrs Bright and Virginia departed and Richard was surprised to see Ginny turn and wave affectionately to him as her mother closed the gate. This was something he could never remember Ginny doing before and he was touched by it. It was almost as if she knew. He felt a renewed pang at the hurt and worry he would cause everyone. To put it out of his mind he went hurriedly to the phone and rang Ben.

'I'm ready to go now,' he said as soon as Ben had said 'Hello'. 'The sooner the better – no one's about.'

'Give me fifteen minutes,' said Ben, 'I'll see you there. And Richard, have you got a clock?'

'Er – no. I've got my watch, though.'

'I think we may need an alarm clock,' Ben explained. 'It's all right, I'll bring one.

Ben's first question on meeting was: 'Did you have a vision last night?'

'No. It looks as though they may have stopped, doesn't it?'

Ben shook his head with a strange look. 'Don't you believe it,' he said. 'There was a man waiting for me on the stairs this morning. I've never seen this one before. He was young and dark-haired and big built. He was only wearing a shirt and trousers and – I think – sort of boots. He seemed as though he wanted to guide me. His clothes weren't modern, Richard.'

Richard's jaw had dropped open. 'But – but – you can't have seen anyone,' he muttered incredulously. 'Not in broad daylight.'

'He was there,' Ben insisted. 'He beckoned to me. Then, as soon as I stepped on to the stairs, he vanished.'

'Vanished?'

'Yes, just disappeared. You know, like a phantom.'

'W-were you frightened?' Richard stammered.

'No. Strangely enough, I wasn't. He seemed so harmless in the daylight.'

'Let's get the ring,' Richard said urgently. 'We've got to get going.'

'Who's going to carry it?' Ben asked subtly as they ran to the shed.

'I don't know. We'd better toss for it. Unless you want it?'

'No, I don't want it. O.K., we'll toss. The winner looks after all the money and the loser . . .' He didn't finish.

They found the place easily enough. Richard dug out

the ring with his pen-knife. He left it lying on the ground as he took a coin from his pocket. 'Call,' he said.

'Heads.'

The coin came down heads. 'Oh hell,' said Richard. Ben took all the money. Richard bent to pick up the ring, but suddenly he straightened up. He had seen something from the corner of his eye. Slowly he turned his head. A young dark man was standing by the door of the shed. He was exactly as Ben had described him. Richard nudged Ben and pointed with a trembling finger. Ben swung round.

'What?' he gasped.

The figure vanished. 'The – the same man,' Richard croaked. 'Standing by the shed. The one *you* saw. He was there, just for a moment. And he was smiling at me!'

Ben said nothing. Richard grabbed the ring and they ran back to their bikes. As they cycled from the garden the house-martins were darting about, as busy as ever. One of the nests under the houses eaves, perhaps badly constructed, rocked considerably as an adult bird alighted on it with food in its beak for the nestlings. All at once part of it broke away and dropped to the ground where it smashed, spilling out a half-fledged youngster which was instantly killed.

'Oh look, poor little thing,' said Ben.

Richard gulped, his nerves were still on edge. 'Maybe it's an omen,' he whispered. 'What can it mean?'

—11—
London Bound

'Where did you leave your note?' Ben asked as they cycled to Hallenden Station. He had worked out the times of the trains with his father's timetable.

'On my bed,' Richard replied. 'How about you?'

'I put mine behind the old clock in our dining-room.'

'*Behind* the clock?' Richard queried. 'Are you sure it'll be found?'

'Oh yes. It's a very old clock and my father winds it up every night.'

Richard frowned. 'Your parents are going to be in suspense for a long while then,' he remarked. 'I think my note will be discovered quite early.'

'Not too early, I hope,' Ben said. 'I say, I hope you didn't give any clues as to where we're going?'

'Of course not,' Richard said indignantly.

As they swung into the station yard they saw Donald Bone approaching from another direction. The station had been a regular haunt of the man's, along with Hallenden High Street, ever since he had suspected the boys possessed the Machy relic. He had been expecting them to make a move and it was quite obvious to Ben and Richard that he had seen them and intended to keep them in view.

'You look after the bikes and the bags,' Ben said

sharply. 'I'll get the tickets.' He leapt off, leaving Richard to hold his bike and rushed into the ticket hall. There was a short queue. He was preparing to ask for return tickets to Tenby when he saw Bone come into the building. The man mustn't know where they were going. When he got to the ticket-office window Ben said, 'Two half-fare return tickets to London, please.'

Bone had joined the queue and was listening hard.

'Day return?' asked the railman.

Ben was flustered. 'Er – er – what other sort is there?' he enquired.

'Are you coming back today?' the railman asked patiently.

'N-no, probably not,' Ben muttered. He hadn't expected any problems with tickets.

'Well, do you want period returns then?' the man's voice could be clearly heard by everyone in the queue.

'Yes, please,' said Ben in a small voice. He knew Bone would have heard everything. He paid the money out from his store and was just taking the tickets when he remembered their bikes. 'Can we take our bikes on the train?' he asked.

'Yes, yes. See the guard when the train comes in. He'll be in one of the middle carriages.'

Ben heaved a sigh of relief and ran back outside without looking at Bone. 'I had to book to London,' he gasped as Richard waved his arm, pointing to where Bone was standing in the booking-hall. 'I didn't want him to know exactly where we're heading. But he heard everything. He knows we're taking our bikes and he knows we're going away for a time. The man in the ticket office made me say what sort of tickets we wanted.'

'What do you mean?' Richard asked, puzzled. Ben explained. 'Oh no,' Richard groaned. 'He'll be following us the whole time!'

'We might shake him off in London,' Ben said without a lot of confidence. 'We've got bikes and he hasn't.'

'I don't fancy cycling in London traffic,' said Richard.

'We've *got* to,' Ben insisted. 'We have to get to Paddington.'

'I hope you know the way,' Richard murmured.

'Naturally,' Ben answered a little cockily. 'I've worked out our route from Dad's *A-Z*. And I've got it all written down.'

They wheeled their bikes on to the platform. They had slung their bags over the handlebars. 'What time's the train?' Richard asked.

Ben glanced at his watch. 'In about five minutes.'

Bone stood watching them, farther along the platform. He had a sardonic grin on his face.

'We'll make sure we keep well away from *him*,' Richard commented.

The train arrived. Ben located the guard and they lifted their bikes into the carriage where indicated and secured them. They unloaded their bags and went to find seats. They didn't know for sure if Bone had boarded the train; however, he was nowhere to be seen on the station. The train moved off. Richard and Ben got into a compartment with plenty of other passengers. They walked through it to check that Bone hadn't chosen the same one, then sat in the end seats.

The journey to London took about seventy minutes. While they were travelling the friends discussed the strange vision they had both had of the young dark-haired man.

'Who is he? What has he to do with Mr Mackie?' Ben wanted to know.

'He must be one of the earlier Machys,' Richard deduced. 'An ancestor who, perhaps, died young. I told you, in one of my "dreams" or whatever they are, I saw lots of different people in a group, some in one sort of dress, some in another. You know – from various periods in history. They were all bound together by their interest in the missing relic. And they were urging me on to the railway station. It all links up, doesn't it, Ben?'

Ben nodded thoughtfully. After some moments' silence he said, 'Well, I only hope, now we're doing what they want, that they leave us alone.'

The train pulled in to Charing Cross Station. The boys made their way back to their bikes. Donald Bone was standing waiting for them.

'Going to enjoy a day out in London?' he asked them sarcastically.

'None of your business,' Ben answered boldly.

'Isn't it though? Oh, now I think you might find you're wrong there.'

The boys got their bikes unfastened and were soon out on the station platform. Bone hung around, then followed them, glowering.

'What do we do now?' Richard whispered.

'Ignore him,' said Ben.

'No, I mean when we get out of the station.'

'We head for Piccadilly, then along Piccadilly to Hyde Park Corner, then we have to – '

'All right, all right,' said Richard. 'I'll just do as you do.'

When they had pushed their bikes through the ticket barrier and into the station concourse Bone sidled up to them again. It seemed he had decided to adopt different tactics regarding them. 'Are you kids hungry?' he enquired. 'I'll buy you some breakfast, if you like.'

Ben and Richard were taken aback for a moment. Then Richard said, 'We've had breakfast, thank you.'

'Oh go on, how about a Coke and a hamburger?' Bone

wheedled. 'I know what boys of your age are like. Always hungry.'

'What's the catch?' Ben asked distrustfully.

'No catch,' Bone assured him. 'I'm just trying to be friendly.'

'Why? You haven't been, before.'

'Well, we can all co-operate with each other, can't we?' Bone suggested slyly. 'Makes things much easier.'

'Oh no,' said Richard. 'We know what your game is. Leave us alone, we've got to go.'

'Go? Where are you going? I'll come with you. Boys of your age shouldn't wander around a big city unaccompanied.'

'Push off!' Richard shouted at him angrily. 'Come on, Ben, get a move on. You're supposed to be the navigator.' He was annoyed at the way Ben appeared to be dawdling as though he had been tempted by the man's offer.

'Sorry.' Ben hurried to make amends. 'That's the Strand.' He pointed to the busy road outside the station. 'We have to go towards Trafalgar Square.'

Richard looked at the traffic; the taxis, the buses, roaring past. He and Ben had cycled amongst motor traffic countless times at home and were quite used to it. But that was nothing compared to this. They heard Bone's voice again.

'You're surely not going to attempt to cycle through that lot?' He was hoping to frighten them. 'Drivers in London are careless of boys on bikes. They won't be expecting to see any. You'll put your lives in danger. Think of your parents.'

His words had an effect on Richard who found it difficult to ignore them, much as he despised the man.

'Why go on with all this?' Bone cajoled them. 'Give me the piece of metal' – he deliberately sought to downgrade the ring in the boy's eyes – 'and give yourselves peace of mind.'

Richard almost felt inclined to hand the object over. But Ben now saw Bone for the hypocrite he was. 'Never!' he cried fiercely. 'You've stolen enough already!' He mounted his bike and, threading his way through the line of taxis outside the station, pedalled over the cobbles down to the Strand. Richard followed him hastily. Bone pursued them.

'Where are you going?' he roared after them. 'You'll regret this, by God you will!'

When Richard didn't show up for lunch Mrs Bright was naturally worried. He never missed his meals. She took Ginny with her and scoured the streets of the town. Her husband had taken his lunch to the shop which he quite often did if he was very busy. She alerted him to the situation and then went quickly back home to see if Richard had turned up.

As they passed the House of the Martins Ginny pointed to it and said to her mother, 'Aren't you going to look in there?'

Mrs Bright stopped. 'Mr Mackie's old house?'

Ginny nodded. 'Richard and Ben were always playing there, Mummy.'

They went into the garden and round to the back of the house. They saw nothing but a skinny white cat which was eating the remains of an unfortunate fledgling close to one of the walls. It ran away at their approach. Ginny went to look in through the windows. She stood on tiptoe and peeped in. The house was as silent and empty as a tomb. There was a notice in one window about the forthcoming auction of the contents.

Mrs Bright prepared to leave. 'It doesn't look to me as if anyone's been here for a long time,' she said.

'Wait a minute, Mummy.' Ginny ran down the steps to the cellar door which she tried and found locked.

'What are you doing?'

Ginny wondered whether to explain about the cellar; that she and Richard had been in there and had been warned off by a strange man. But Richard and she had made a pact not to tell anyone about that. 'Nothing,' she answered. 'I just thought I'd see if that door would open.'

'Come on, Ginny. Richard may be back by now.'

But of course he wasn't. Mrs Bright ran upstairs to see if he was in his bedroom. And then she found the note. It was half-past two.

Richard and Ben had found the traffic that was roaring around Trafalgar Square too much for them. They wheeled their bikes across roads and along pavements until they came to Lower Regent Street. Ben consulted his route notes. 'This leads to Piccadilly,' he informed his friend. 'Then it's left at Piccadilly Circus. We can cycle a bit now. It's not so bad.'

The boys looked round. Bone had been following them at a discreet distance all along. He didn't want to make a scene with so many people around. The boys got on their bikes and cautiously began to pedal up the incline to the Circus. They had to wait at the traffic lights and then, with Ben leading the way, they turned into the bus lane which led westwards along Piccadilly. It was after twelve o'clock and both boys were beginning to feel hungry. A bus went past them and hooted. They were both a bit scared and wondered if they were doing something they shouldn't. But there was nothing for it but to continue. Bone was running now, along the pavement of Piccadilly, dodging the crowds and trying to keep up. Eventually the bus lane ended and soon Ben and

Richard found themselves at Hyde Park Corner. Here they had a bit of luck. There was a cycle track through the park all the way to Marble Arch, which was their next destination point.

'I'm starving,' said Richard. 'What did you bring to eat?'

'Tinned food mostly,' Ben replied.

'I've got a packet of biscuits,' said Richard. 'I'll get them out.' He pulled them from his bag, together with the cheese. They munched these companionably as they progressed along the cycle track. It was warm, the park was green and shady and their spirits lifted. They came to a kiosk selling snacks and drinks. They stocked up on canned drinks, crisps, more biscuits, sausage rolls and chocolate bars. As they were about to get going again they were surprised to see Donald Bone labouring along the track at a ragged sort of jog.

'Oh no!' Richard exclaimed. 'I thought we'd got rid of him.'

They put on a spurt, hoping to lose him for good. At Marble Arch Ben consulted his notes again. 'Edgware Road, Praed Street, Paddington Station,' he read out. 'Richard, we're almost there.'

Both boys were parched but they didn't dare stop there and then for a drink. They found a signpost which showed them the way to Edgware Road. Twenty minutes later, at half-past one, they neared the station.

By half-past three Mrs Bright had spoken to Ben's mother on the phone. She had read Richard's note out to her. After a search Mrs Tompkins rang back in tears, saying her son hadn't even had the thought to leave one himself. The two mothers were frantic. They couldn't imagine what had got into their boys. Some hare-brained adventure, putting themselves at grave risk and worrying everyone half to death! Neither women knew which of the two was the perpetrator of this stupidity. Mrs Bright was inclined to think it must be the madcap Ben Tompkins but of course she had no proof. Mrs Tompkins rang her husband at the bank. He told her to inform the police. She answered briskly that she had already done so and an officer was due to call round shortly.

In the end it was the boys' sisters who were able to throw some light on the escapade. Ginny had been bursting to tell about the Mackie house incident and at last, despite her pledge, could hold it back no longer. She was desperately worried about Richard and really believed he was in some danger from the dark-faced man whose name she didn't know. The story came out, worrying Mrs Bright even further. At about the same time Angela Tompkins came home from a friend's to find her mother in tears. She immediately found out the cause of it and then began, herself, to put two and two together. She recalled Ben's asking about the train journey to Wales and explained everything to her mother. The only trouble was, she couldn't remember exactly where in Wales he had asked about.

'Wales!' cried Mrs Tompkins in anguish. 'My God, they've gone mad, the pair of them. What on earth has possessed them to do this?' She got on the phone again to Valerie Bright and between them they pieced together the evidence. Mrs Bright had remembered Richard's nightmare and the two mothers began to see that their sons' disturbed nights and recent moodiness had somehow been brought on by an event connected with what they called the House of the Martins.

'There's been some sort of experience there,' Mrs Tompkins declared. 'Something strange. I'm sure of it.'

'I think you're right,' said Richard's mother. 'It's a sinister sort of place in a way and I think the boys have frightened themselves to death by it. This crazy journey of theirs must have resulted from that.'

Mrs Tompkins suggested that she should come round and talk to the police officer with her and Mrs Bright left at once, taking Ginny with her.

While all this was happening Richard and Ben were on the two o'clock train to Swansea, though they had found unsuspected difficulties getting themselves there when they had reached Paddington. They had lost track of Bone who had trailed them as far as the Edgware Road before they had slipped out of sight. However, more by luck than judgement, he had decided to go to the nearest railway terminus which happened to be Paddington. He didn't see the boys board the Swansea train but he managed, by dint of masquerading as an irate relative, to winkle out of the booking-office staff where the two boys were travelling. Thus he only had to wait for the next service before he was once again in hot pursuit.

—— 12 ——
A Long Train Journey

The boys' plan had nearly come to grief at the first hurdle. They had no idea their fares to Wales would be so expensive. Once again there was confusion over what sort of ticket they wanted. Ben pretended they were going down to stay with an aunt for a few days to allay possible suspicion of two young boys travelling on their own. They were advised to buy saver returns which cost them £31.00 for the two. Ben could hardly believe it. Then he asked about putting their bikes on the train.

'Have you paid the reserve fee?' the man asked.

'W-what's that?' stammered Ben.

'You have to reserve a place for bikes on inter-city trains in advance. There's limited space.'

'Oh dear, we didn't know that.'

The man shook his head dubiously. 'Well, you'll have to take pot luck then, but you may find there's no room.'

Ben and Richard were lucky. The train wasn't over-crowded and the guard took pity on them. They sank into their seats with relief. They were quite excited about a long train journey, which was a new experience for them. They were told they had to change at Swansea for the train to Tenby. From there they would cycle to Manorbier. They had discovered they wouldn't reach Tenby until nearly seven o'clock in the evening. It would still be light then but the boys knew they would have to stay at least one night away and neither of them were terribly happy about that. Richard had absolutely no idea how to go about finding shelter but Ben was a bit more competent. His family sometimes went touring, and often his father booked them in at bed and breakfast accommodation in the more remote parts of the countryside. He explained to Richard how this worked. He was fairly confident that they would find somewhere without too much difficulty, and Richard was content to leave the arrangements to him. However there was the question of money.

'What will it cost?' he asked as they nibbled at the contents of one of their crisp packets.

Ben took a swig from a can of lemonade. 'I'm not sure. Not a lot for one night, I shouldn't think. We'll share a room.'

'How much have we got left?'

Ben had already counted up. 'Seventeen pounds and a few pence,' he answered.

'Is that all?'

'Yes, it should just about last us out.'

'D'you really think so?' Richard persisted.

'It'll have to,' Ben said grimly.

In Hallenden the police sergeant asked the boys' families a lot of questions and made careful notes. He didn't stay long. He tried to reassure them that it shouldn't be too difficult to trace two twelve-year-old boys who were biking around South Wales in the Swansea area (Angela had remembered that much) without supervision. He had full and intricate descriptions of the boys, their clothes and their bikes too. Inquiries would be instituted immediately, he promised them, and Mrs Bright and Mrs Tompkins watched him depart, both feeling considerably heartened now an officer of the law had taken control of affairs.

Mrs Tompkins rang her husband at the bank to report on the interview and Mrs Bright took Ginny home again where she found Geoffrey Bright waiting for her in an agitated state. He had closed his shop early, unable to concentrate on business.

'Stupid silly boys,' he said after hearing the latest news. 'I would never have believed this of Richard.' He read Richard's message through for the twentieth time. 'I just can't comprehend what's got into him. I always said that Ben – '

'No, it's not Ben's fault more than Richard's,' Valerie Bright interrupted. 'Don't you see, they can't help themselves? They're frightened of something and they're trying to run away from it.'

'To Wales? Why, in Heaven's name?'

'Only they can tell us. There's some connection with Wales and that house.'

A light began to dawn at the back of Mr Bright's mind. 'The Mackie house, isn't it? Half a minute, there was something about a Welsh connection in his Will; Todd told me that. What was it now? Yes, yes, I know . . . the old man left his belongings to some charity down in Wales. But how could the boys be involved in that? It doesn't make sense.'

Richard and Ben reached Swansea and changed trains, offloading their bikes from the London train to the one bound for Tenby. Ben bought a map of the area from the station bookstall. They were well on the way to the seaside resort while, back at Hallenden, the policeman was just leaving the Tompkins' house. By now the boys were very, very hungry and, although they tucked into their sausage rolls and chocolate, these didn't suffice.

*

Since leaving home Richard hadn't once taken the Machy ring out of his pocket. He hardly dared touch it in case it might provoke one of the family ancestors to suddenly materialize, like the genie of the lamp. He hated having the ornament about his person and he really was genuinely fearful of its mysterious power.

The journey to Tenby, although it was through some interesting scenery, seemed to the two boys to last for ever. The train twisted and turned through the Welsh countryside and they felt as if they had been sitting on a train for days. They had been travelling solidly for over nine hours by the time they reached Tenby. It was nearly seven o'clock in the evening and it was raining. They clambered wearily out of their seats and went through the compartments to collect their bikes. The guard looked at them curiously.

'You lads have come a long way,' he said. 'Holidaying in Tenby, are you?'

'No, Manorbier,' Ben replied instinctively, then groaned inwardly.

'Manorbier? That's quite a way. You're not going on your own, surely?'

'Oh no,' Ben lied. 'Our friends are meeting us at the station.'

The guard nodded but looked as if he couldn't quite make up his mind if he believed them or not. 'Well, have a good time,' he said. 'The weather's not giving you much of a welcome, though.'

It wasn't. Ben and Richard reached the station exit with glum expressions as they saw the rain slanting across the station forecourt. It drummed angrily on the roofs and bonnets of the few taxis parked there. They pulled out their anoraks and got into them, yanking the hoods over their heads.

Richard felt very forlorn. 'We can't cycle through this,' he grumbled. 'We'd be soaked in no time.'

'Well, we can't stay here,' Ben remonstrated. 'We have to find someone to put us up. It's getting late and we need to do that straight away.'

Richard looked around him. The weather, the station, the whole place at that time of the day and in the teeming rain looked infinitely depressing. 'Oh hell, Ben, I wish we'd never come.'

Ben looked bleak. 'So do I,' he muttered. 'It's been a really awful day.'

Richard was a bit taken aback. 'Oh. I thought you were enjoying yourself earlier on?'

'The first part was all right,' Ben answered. 'But I thought the journey would never come to an end. I'm so tired.'

'Me too,' Richard agreed.

Deep Welsh tones broke into their conversation. 'D'you kids want a lift somewhere?' It was a taxi driver calling to them. He'd been watching them for some time.

'N-no, thanks,' Richard answered. 'We're cycling. Er . . . to an aunt's,' he finished hurriedly.

'Well done,' Ben whispered.

Now the boys realized they could loiter no longer. They zipped up their anoraks and set off towards the town. Immediately they saw there was no shortage of 'B & B' signs. These hung outside all sorts of houses, some modest, some large. However a lot of them had an accompanying sign: 'No vacancies'. It was the height of the holiday season. Eventually they found a house which looked promising. It was small and neat and had a lovely cottage garden. The name over the door read 'The Haven'. The boys stopped pedalling. The rain beat relentlessly against their faces.

'That looks nice,' said Ben. 'Shall we try it?'

'Yes, we'd better. Er – Ben?'

'What?'

'What are we going to tell them? I mean, we'll have to invent a story, won't we? They're bound to wonder what we're up to, on our own down here.'

'Yes, I don't suppose the "aunt" bit will do any more, will it? Any ideas?'

'We could say we're lost,' suggested Richard.

'No, that's no good, Rich. They'd only want to fire all sorts of questions at us. Where we're heading, why we're by ourselves, all that sort of business.'

'How about telling the truth?'

'Don't be daft. You can just imagine them swallowing all the old Mackie stuff, I *don't* think.'

'I didn't mean the exact truth, Ben. But we could say we're supposed to be cycling to a relation's at Manorbier and, because of the weather, we phoned up and they said to find a place overnight and then go on in the morning.'

'Hey, that's not at all bad,' Ben said admiringly.

Suddenly the boys saw a lace curtain twitched to one side and an elderly woman peer out at them from the front window of the house.

'Come on, she looks as though she wants to help,' said Richard. He pushed the gate open and they wheeled their bikes up the garden path. The door was opened before they reached it.

'I wondered when you were going to come in,' said the elderly woman. She was short, grey-haired and stout. She had a warm friendly voice. 'You don't want to hang about in this weather. Where are your mum and dad?'

'They're not with us,' Richard answered quickly. 'We're on holiday, you see. We're supposed to be going to Manorbier but Auntie – er – Barbara said to leave it until tomorrow because of the weather.'

'Yes, she told us there were lots of places to stay in Tenby,' Ben backed him up.

'Why Tenby?' asked the woman.

'We've just got off the train,' Ben explained.

'Well, come along in, come along in,' she invited them. She didn't sound in the least suspicious. 'Put your bicycles over there.' She pointed to the car port at the side of the house. There was no car.

Inside the hall she relieved them of their wet coats and gave these a brisk shake on the porch. 'These need drying,' she said, 'and so do you, by the look of you. Go into the bathroom and rub yourselves down. You'll find clean towels on the towel rail.'

The boys relaxed, only too glad at last to have an adult assume command. While they washed and dried themselves the lady bustled in. 'Your room's across the passage – the one with the twin beds. Go and get yourselves sorted out. I'm Mrs Stephens. You can call me Dorothy. What are your names?'

'I'm Richard and this is Ben,' said Richard.

'Are you hungry?'

The boys nodded vigorously.

'I'll expect you down in half an hour,' said Dorothy. 'Make yourselves at home.' She seemed to be enjoying herself. 'There's no one else here so you've got the run of the place. I'm sorry the phone's out of order otherwise you could tell your auntie where you are. Never mind, you'll be all right with me. Do you like fish? Yes? Good.' She hurried off to begin cooking. She appeared to be delighted to be busy doing something for someone. It was clear she lived alone and Richard and Ben thought she might be lonely. Soon they could smell the aroma of cooking food wafting up the stairs to them from the kitchen.

'Ooh, real food at last,' Ben enthused. 'I can't wait!'

Richard glanced at his watch. 'You'll have to survive a bit longer,' he joked. The rain still dashed against the windows. 'Gosh, I hope it's not like this tomorrow,' he added.

Fifteen minutes later they were attacking steaming platefuls of fried cod, chips and peas. Dorothy watched them eat with gusto. She stood with her arms folded, nodding and smiling with approval. 'That's the way, I like to see boys with a good appetite,' she said. The fish was followed by apple pie and custard.

'Whereabouts in Manorbier are you staying?' she asked presently. 'I know some folk there.'

Richard and Ben stopped in mid-mouthful. Here was a problem.

'Er – we – we haven't actually been there before,' Ben spluttered. 'My aunt lives near the – um – church, you know.'

'The Baptist Church?'

'I'm not sure,' Ben confessed.

'Oh, you'll like Manorbier. It's a lovely place. There's a castle and a big bay where you can bathe, you know, and cliff walks.'

Ben nodded enthusiastically. He didn't want to have to deal with any more tricky questions. Dorothy prattled on while the boys finished their meal. She took the things into the kitchen to wash up.

'Ben,' Richard hissed as soon as her back was turned, 'we didn't ask her how much we have to pay!'

Ben clapped a hand to his mouth. 'Oh no!' he muttered. 'We're stuck now, we'll have to stay here.'

Dorothy came back shortly and invited the boys to watch television with her. They didn't really want to, they were both exhausted, but she was being so nice to them they felt they couldn't refuse.

'Er, Mrs – um – Dorothy, you didn't tell us what you

charge,' Ben said awkwardly as he and Richard were directed to a comfortable sofa.

'Oh, you won't have to break the bank,' she joked. 'I ask ten pounds per person for a double room and breakfast but, seeing as you're only kids like, I'll make it eight pounds.'

'That's very kind,' said Ben, relieved they could pay their way. But Richard wasn't relieved at all. He knew they would have to pay for their supper as well and his heart sank as he realized that they couldn't possibly have enough. There was no way of drawing Ben's attention to this there and then but, as soon as they could do so with politeness, the friends excused themselves and went to bed. Both of them had been dozing on and off for an hour or more despite the television and Dorothy's quick Welsh voice describing her family's life history.

Once they were in their room Richard was at last able to tell Ben he had miscalculated.

'She didn't say anything about paying for our meal, she only mentioned breakfast,' Ben remarked. His family had never had an evening meal at such an establishment and he wasn't sure of his ground.

'You didn't ask, that's why she didn't tell us,' Richard said. 'She's bound to want us to pay. Why would she give us it for nothing?'

'Well, we can't pay, can we?' Ben replied moodily. He thought Richard was putting the blame on him for being careless.

'We'll have to give her what we can,' Richard said, 'but then we shall be skint and what do we do about food tomorrow?'

'Perhaps we won't need any. You get a brilliant breakfast usually at these B & B places and then we've still got some of our own food left.'

'Yes, but suppose we have to stay away another night?'

Ben couldn't answer that and the boys got into bed silently, their heads full of horrible ideas of being stranded and destitute, sleeping rough and going hungry. They didn't talk any more but it was a long time before either of them got to sleep.

Alan Tompkins replaced the clock on the mantelpiece and, with visibly shaking hands slit open the envelope he had found behind it. His son's note was excessively brief:

'*Gone away for a while with Richard. Will telephone when I can. Back as soon as poss. Love, Ben.*'

Mr Tompkins swallowed hard as he looked at the Edwardian clock. Eleven-ten. The police had so far only been able to report that two boys with bicycles answering to Ben's and Richard's descriptions had bought tickets at Paddington Station. Station staff had been able to confirm that they had been travelling to Tenby, and that an angry relative had bought a ticket to the same destination shortly afterwards. This naturally alarmed the parents. Meanwhile enquiries were continuing. Ben's father heaved a deep sigh and took Ben's note upstairs to his wife. 'Ben wasn't totally heartless,' he muttered as he handed it to her.

Jane Tompkins' eyes greedily devoured the boyish handwriting. 'Oh, why *hasn't* he phoned?' she wailed. 'They must be in some trouble, Alan. I know it. Perhaps they've been kidnapped.'

'Now, we mustn't jump to conclusions,' Mr Tompkins cautioned, trying to soothe her. 'It can only be a matter of time before the police locate them.'

'But who is this "relative" we're told about?' his wife demanded with anguish. 'They've got involved with somebody – God knows who.'

'That must be a mistake. I think the railway people were confused. They deal with thousands of people every day and I'm quite certain that – '

'How can you be certain?' Mrs Tompkins cried. 'You're no more certain than I am. I just have this dreadful feeling that they've been kidnapped.'

Donald Bone arrived at Tenby a couple of hours after the boys. He didn't think they would have got much farther that night and he set himself to look for clues in the little town. He had no luggage with him. He gritted his teeth in the driving rain, bent his head and walked towards the centre. He intended to look in restaurants and places of amusement along the seafront. But, as it turned out, he didn't have to go that far. He walked right past Mrs Stephens' house and there he saw the bikes in the car port as plain as day. It was the best clue he could have asked for. He backtracked and noticed the 'Vacancies' sign. He needed accommodation himself. But before he knocked on the door he examined the bikes closely. He recognized them with ease. He had had them in his sights enough that day to make no mistake. And he was clever enough to realize that, if he could recognize them, then so could anyone else who had been given a sufficiently accurate description. The police, of course, would have been alerted. So he tiptoed to the back of the car port where there was an old tarpaulin folded up. Evidently it had been used to protect the car that once had been parked there. He carefully spread the tarpaulin over Ben's and Richard's bikes. There was no point in having the boys under the wing of the police before he had got the valuable object away from them. And he was determined to get it by whatever means.

Bone knocked on Mrs Stephens' door.

'Yes?' Dorothy asked dubiously, eyeing his scruffy figure.

'Have you a room by any chance?'

'Well – ' She hesitated.

'It's a dreadful night and I haven't been able to find anywhere else,' Bone whispered persuasively.

'Would it be just for one night?'

'I think that'd be all I require,' said the man with an ingratiating smile. 'Don't you have a lovely house?'

'Thank you,' said Dorothy. She looked him over again. Her good nature overcame her prejudices. 'Oh very well, then,' she said. 'You'd better come in out of the rain.'

—13—
Unwelcome Company

Bone stepped into the hall. He had no head covering and his dark hair was plastered to his scalp with wet. Water streamed down his neck and dripped on to the carpet. His dark features looked a little sinister.

'Haven't you any bags or anything?' Dorothy asked. She began to feel a little nervous.

'No, nothing,' Bone said glibly. 'I travel light – everything in my pockets.'

'Oh. Oh, I see.' (Dorothy didn't see at all). 'You'll have eaten, of course?'

'No. No, I haven't.' Bone rubbed his hands together at the prospect of a meal.

'Oh dear,' said Dorothy. 'It's really too late now for me to begin cooking again. There's a pub just down the road from here that does food. Bar meals like. They're quite good. It's called the "Robin Inn".'

Bone shivered. 'I don't think I could face going out in that weather again,' he said as Dorothy led him upstairs to his room. It was just across the landing from the boys' room. 'Haven't you got a bit of bread and cheese or cold meat or something?'

'I'll see what I can do,' Dorothy answered. 'It *is* nasty out there. Now, here you are, I think there's everything you want here. D'you want me to hang your wet things in the airing cupboard?'

Bone removed his coat without a word and handed it to her. Then he asked in a low voice, 'Do you have other guests here?'

'Just two lads,' Dorothy told him. 'On their way to an auntie's at Manorbier.' Bone started involuntarily at the name. 'They had to find shelter tonight like you. Lucky I was empty.'

Bone closed his bedroom door behind her, smiling grimly. Food first, he told himself, then later on when the old girl was in bed he could do a little exploring . . .

The boys hadn't been asleep long. Now they slept on, innocent of the threat that hung over them in the otherwise friendly atmosphere of 'The Haven'. Late in the night (or so it seemed to him) Richard was wakened by rustlings and clickings just outside their door. He had no reason to fear any intrusion and he lay, still half asleep, without moving as Bone carefully turned the door handle from outside. The door opened without a sound. Richard thought he heard some muffled sounds in the room but dismissed them as nothing more than Ben turning over in his sleep. He was just drifting back into slumber when there was a thud. He sat up. Bone was at the foot of the bed, his hand in Richard's bag as he searched for the Machy ring. The room was very dark and, in his haste, Bone had knocked a pile of clothes on to the floor from a chair by the bed. He cursed silently and froze as Richard stared at him. The boy thought he saw a shadowy figure but, suspecting another vision, said nothing. With a racing heart Richard watched to see what would happen. Bone didn't move and so the two stared at each other in the darkness, not knowing what move to make next. Then there was a noise from outside the room. Mrs Stephens was stirring. Bone slowly lowered Richard's bag to the floor and stole out of the room. Just as he reached the landing Dorothy, on her way to the bathroom, flicked on a light and Richard, for the briefest moment, saw Bone illuminated in the passage before he dived back into his own bedroom.

Richard gave a little cry, then leant over and shook Ben awake. 'Ben, Ben,' he gasped in horrified disbelief, 'he's here! In this house!'

Ben struggled back to consciousness. 'What? What's up?' he muttered.

'Bone! He's here, he came into our room. Look, our door's open.'

Ben sat bolt upright. Then the initial shock subsided and he sank back down again. 'Oh, Richard, don't be silly. How could he be? We lost him in London. You've had another vision, that's all.'

'I haven't had a vision,' Richard replied angrily. 'He's here, Ben. Now. I don't know how but he's here.'

Ben realized Richard was telling the truth. 'The – ring,' he murmured.

Richard turned on the light and leapt out of bed. He closed the door and then turned to the pile of clothes that had fallen on the floor. He found his jeans and quickly reassured himself the ring was still in a pocket.

'Thank goodness,' said Ben as Richard flourished it at him.

'Bone was disturbed,' Richard said. 'We were lucky this time.' He shuddered as he pictured again Bone standing at the foot of the bed, motionless, watching him silently. 'We've got to get out of here, Ben, get away from him.'

'How? When?' Ben stammered. 'He'll be waiting for us.'

'Not if we leave now.'

Ben glanced at his alarm clock. It was one o'clock. 'Now!' he hissed. 'What on earth are you talking about? It's the middle of the night.'

'Of course it is,' said Richard. 'Just the time to get away from him. He won't expect that. He can't come in here again, he knows we've spotted him. So he'll be waiting at breakfast.'

'But – but – it's pitch-dark,' Ben protested. 'We don't know where we are or where to go. We'll lose ourselves. And – and – it's dangerous, Richard.'

Richard saw sense. 'O.K.,' he agreed. 'We'll wait until it's light. Bone will be sleeping probably. We'll steal downstairs and let ourselves out. You've got the map. We can work out where we have to go.'

'But we can't just walk out on Dorothy like that,' Ben maintained. 'We owe her money and – '

'We'll leave the money,' Richard interrupted testily. 'It doesn't matter what she thinks. This is more important. Perhaps we can leave a note to explain, *I* don't know. But we've got to avoid Bone and get the ring back to Manorbier. That's why we came. We can't fail now or all the Machys who ever lived will come to haunt us.' Richard said this more as a means of convincing Ben than of frightening him. But he half-believed what he was saying and his dire words succeeded in terrifying them both. They cowered together, clasping one another for comfort as though they expected the Fate they had tempted was about to bring swift retribution.

The hours passed slowly. They didn't speak much and, as their minds began to be filled with other thoughts, chiefly about their parents and home, they relaxed despite themselves. Tired as they were they began to nod, and soon both boys lay on their beds sound asleep. They could have slept till breakfast-time had it not been for Dorothy Stephens' pressing need to visit the bathroom every few hours. They woke to her footsteps along the landing and jumped up, thinking they had overslept. Then they looked at the clock. It was five-thirty and the sky was just beginning to pale. They tugged their clothes on, stuffed their possessions into their bags, rinsed their faces with cold water and prepared to leave.

'What about the money?' Ben queried. 'How much shall we leave?'

'Sixteen pounds. That's what she said,' Richard answered. 'Last night's meal replaces breakfast.' They didn't stop to write a message. 'We'll be able to explain some day,' Richard said to comfort their consciences.

They crept downstairs. They didn't dare turn on a light. They used their own torch. Ben left sixteen pounds on the hall table. Surprisingly Dorothy had left the chain off the door. They turned the knob and pulled it open. They were glad to see the rain had ceased during the night. However the garden was saturated. They closed the door quietly behind them and walked softly to the car port. With a shock they saw that Bone had beaten them to it. It seemed the man had expected them to make a move and had forced himself to stay awake. Now he barred their path. An unpleasant sneering smile was on his face as he stood directly in front of their bikes.

'Making an early start, boys?' he murmured sarcastically.

Ben and Richard halted in their tracks. Bone, looking unshaven and bleary-eyed, was a figure of menace in the half-light. Richard's fingers closed round the ring in his pocket.

'What do we do now?' he whispered. 'We can't *walk* to Manorbier.'

Ben pursed his lips. 'We'll have to bluff it out.'

'How?'

'Like this.' Ben raised his voice. 'What have you done with our bikes?'

'Done? I haven't done anything with them,' said Bone. 'They're under here.' He lifted a corner of the tarpaulin.

'Why don't you let us get to them then?' Ben asked in a voice far bolder than he actually felt.

'Am I stopping you?' Bone leered. 'You know what I want. Why don't you play ball with me? What's the good of the thing to you anyway? You can go wherever you want, *I* shan't stand in your way, but you must see that you have to be a bit amenable too.'

'We're taking the heirloom back where it belongs,' Richard said. 'It's not ours and we don't want to keep it. Why else would we be here? It's not yours either, Mr Bone, and you shouldn't prevent us continuing on our journey. You've no right.'

'Oh, I've plenty of right when it's something I want,' Bone assured them. 'Now what's it to be? It's your choice. Are you going to be sensible lads and pass it over or must I take it from you? Because I'll get it, you know, *you* can't stop me.' He laughed derogatorily.

'We'll have to run for it,' Ben whispered to Richard. 'He's bound to follow us. We'll try and lose him, then we can double back and get to the bikes.' Richard nodded. He could see there was no other way. 'Get ready,' said Ben, 'and run as fast as you can when I say "now".'

The boys tensed. They dropped their bags. Bone watched them through narrowed eyes.

'Now!' Ben yelled. The boys shot away out of the garden, and pelted along the street towards the town centre. Bone was momentarily taken by surprise but he soon gave chase.

Ben and Richard had got a good start and both could run very fast. The streets were utterly deserted at that hour; there was no looking for help from passers-by. They ran down a steep hill to the seafront. They could hear Bone's clattering footsteps behind them; they didn't dare pause for breath. The man's longer legs gained on them gradually. Gasping, the boys darted down a side lane. Richard clutched at his side. He had the most awful stitch. Only the thought that the ring was in his pocket made him keep going. But he was in agony and finally he had to stop. Ben ran on.

'Ben!' Richard cried. 'Wait. I've – got a – pain.'

Ben jerked to a halt and spun round. Bone was coming up the lane, his heavy footsteps slowing as he scented triumph.

'You – you take it,' Richard panted. He was spent. Ben trotted back, his chest heaving. As Richard fished in his pocket, Bone accelerated and reached him, grabbing his arms and pinioning him. Richard just had time to toss the ring awkwardly towards Ben. 'Catch!' he shouted hoarsely. The ring spun in the air, Ben dived forward and caught it low down in his right hand. Bone gave Richard's arm a vicious twist but he was too late. Ben was off again, sprinting harder than ever.

'Get to the bikes,' Richard yelled. 'Get away. I'll – join you – later.'

'That's what you think,' Bone snarled angrily, furious at being frustrated.

'I'm no use to you,' Richard panted. 'I haven't got what you want any more.' He was past the stage of being frightened. He knew Bone would have to be careful. The little town would soon be waking up.

'Damn you!' Bone shouted. He too was panting heavily. Ben disappeared into the distance. The man seemed to be irresolute. He held Richard fast but, at the same time, he could see his prize vanishing before his eyes.

'Let go of me.' Richard kicked and struggled frantically but couldn't free himself. 'I'll shout out. Someone's bound to hear me.' He began to call out for help in a piercingly loud voice. Bone caught him by the chin and smothered his mouth with a grubby hand, pressing Richard's head back against his own chest.

'*You won't beat me.*' Bone emphasized each word. There was spite in his voice. 'Your little friend'll soon be back when you fail to turn up. Meanwhile we'll go somewhere a bit less public.' He turned round and began dragging Richard with him, back down the lane to the seafront. He headed for a bus shelter which he judged would be well out of the gaze of any early stirrers. Once inside, he released his grip slightly over Richard's mouth.

'He won't come back,' Richard mumbled awkwardly from behind the man's hand. 'He has the route. He'll go all the way with that ring, you'll never stop him now.' This was pure bravado. Richard didn't really believe for a minute that Ben would do any such thing without him. The first thing he would almost certainly do would be to rouse Mrs Stephens. But Bone, it seemed, had thought of nearly everything.

'He'll have to pump his tyres up first.' He chuckled maliciously. 'I think that might be a bit difficult without a pump.'

Richard's heart sank at the knowledge that their bikes were immobilized. But there was still Dorothy. An overwhelming hatred of the man who held him prisoner suddenly flooded over him and he wrestled like a mad thing, biting deep into one of Bone's fingers. The man shrieked in agony and instantly his vice-like grip slackened. Richard broke free, kicking Bone hard in the shins and dashing away while he had the advantage. During the last few minutes he had had time to regain his breath, also the pain in his side had subsided. He felt fresh and strong and now he ran uphill, heading for his and Ben's starting point. He could hear Bone's roars of fury farther down the hill but Richard was confident he could outdistance him. Bone had received a shock and his pursuit now was laboured. His angry cries grew fainter and fainter. Eventually Richard was able to slow down to only a brisk walk.

Not much after six o'clock he and Ben arrived by differing routes at 'The Haven'. They gave each other relieved hugs and then exchanged accounts of their experiences. Ben had found it difficult retracing his steps since he didn't know Tenby and he had had to approach the house from a strange direction. The boys hastily whipped off the tarpaulin. Sure enough, all four tyres of their bikes were as flat as pancakes.

'The swine!' Ben cursed. His bicycle pump was missing and he went to look for it amongst the odds and ends at the back of the car port. Richard's was gone too. Whilst Ben searched Richard kept a look-out for Bone. The man showed no sign of approaching. Suddenly Ben gave a cry. He had spotted one of the pumps – his own – lying under some garden plants where Bone had evidently thrown it. Soon after, Richard's was found nearby. Richard continued to keep watch while Ben pumped vigorously, first at his own bike's tyres, then moved on to his friend's.

Needless to say all the activity outside her house ultimately woke the owner. At first she was at a loss to account for the children's voices in the garden. Then, when her faculties had fully returned, she heaved herself out of bed and went to her bedroom window which overlooked the road. She saw Richard standing at the gate, his head turning to the left, then to the right, as if he were the onlooker at a very slow tennis match. Then Ben appeared in view. He was wheeling his bike. Instantly, the hour being such an early one, Dorothy suspected the boys of trying to do a bunk without paying her for their stay. She hastily threw her dressing-gown around herself and hurried downstairs. The sixteen pounds lay on the hall table as a witness to her mistrust, and she felt ashamed of herself. But what *were* they doing, going off without their breakfast?

She opened the door. Richard and Ben, their bags dangling once more from their bicycle handlebars, were just about to pedal away.

'Boys! Boys!' she called pleadingly. 'Wherever are you going? You've got no breakfast inside you!'

For a moment Richard and Ben looked at her regretfully. They would have dearly loved to wait and eat breakfast. But of course that was impossible.

'The man,' Richard mumbled, 'the one you put up. He came into our room last night . . . We're afraid of him. He's after us.'

Dorothy misinterpreted his remarks. She imagined all sorts of horrible things. 'What? My God, he'll have me to answer to then,' she said fiercely and began to go back inside, thinking Bone was asleep upstairs.

'He's not there, Dorothy,' Richard called her back. 'He's in the town somewhere. He tried to prevent us getting away. We can't stop to explain now . . .' The boys pressed down on their pedals.

'Wait! Wait!' Dorothy screeched. She ran back and collected up the money they had left her. She ran out to them in her night attire. 'Take it,' she ordered them. 'I can't accept any of it.' She felt responsible for what had happened. 'In my house,' she wailed. She was close to tears. 'I'll get on to the police as soon as I'm dressed. Oh, what a terrible state of affairs. You poor lambs!'

'We're all right, honest,' said Ben. 'You mustn't give us it *all*, you know,' he said, referring to the money. 'You gave us our meal last night.'

'Oh, I'd give you much, much more to put things right,' she half-sobbed. 'How could I have let him in? Please, dear, take it. And get to your auntie's quickly. I shan't be able to rest. Oh! the horrible man!' For the moment she had entirely overlooked the fact that Bone *had* left without giving her a penny. Her mind was full of far worse offences.

Ben took the money back reluctantly. The lady gave them both a smacking kiss. 'You can tell your auntie to ring Mrs Powell when you get there. Mrs Powell's my neighbour. In case my phone's still not working. Her number's 2622. Promise me you will. I won't get any peace till I know. Promise me!'

'Of course we promise,' said Ben. They gave Dorothy a wave and set off. There was still no sign of Bone.

When he thought they were out of earshot Richard said, 'Keep your eyes peeled, Ben. I know he's lurking somewhere. He's sure to try and stop us.'

Ben gritted his teeth. 'Let him try,' he growled. 'We'll run him down!'

─14─
The End of the Trail

Strangely, as the boys cycled through Tenby, there was no evidence of Bone. They steeled themselves each metre of the way to deal with his sudden appearance from one quarter or another. But he didn't appear. They put the town behind them and, following Ben's map, took the A4139 to Penally. At that time of the morning they had the road to themselves and, once they felt reasonably safe again, they began to enjoy themselves. The air was fresh and brisk after the downpour of the previous night, the sun shone and the sea, over to their left, sparkled brilliantly. The only thing was, they were appallingly hungry.

'We'll stop at a café,' Ben said with the confidence borne of the seventeen pounds in his pocket. 'We'll have cereal and toast and marmalade and eggs and bacon and – and – tomatoes and everything.'

Richard drooled at the picture he conjured up. Breakfast dominated their minds now that Bone seemed, unaccountably, to be out of the way. But, at the back of both boys' minds, was the nagging worry of how their families would be suffering and that they needed to allay these worries as soon as possible. Ben illustrated the fact that they were thinking alike by saying next, 'When we've had breakfast we'll find a telephone. I promised to phone home as soon as I could.'

'I want to phone too,' Richard confirmed. 'And then, what about Dorothy?'

'Well, we must speak to her neighbour as we said,' Ben answered. 'We can pretend we're at our made-up aunt's.'

They cycled on quietly for a while. Ben was now in charge of the ring as well as the money. He had forgotten to give it back to Richard and Richard hadn't asked. The road went inland for a while and then curved back towards the sea as they approached Penally. It was still only seven o'clock and none of the shops or cafés there were open.

'Let's finish up our crisps and biscuits,' Ben suggested. 'I'm famished. Perhaps somewhere will be open at the next town.'

'Where's that?'

'Lydstep.'

They stopped and pulled all the accessible food that was remaining out of their bags, leaving only the tins where they were. 'Oh, if only we could have stayed a bit longer at Dorothy's!' Richard said ruefully after they had demolished all the packages which had already been half-consumed. 'I can just imagine the sort of breakfast *she* would have given us.'

At Lydstep they sat on a seat in the sun overlooking the sea, counting the minutes to when the cafés opened.

'What do you think happened to Bone?' Richard wondered.

'Don't know and don't care,' Ben retorted. 'We've got rid of him and now the police will be on his tail.'

'You know, I don't want to be a pessimist,' Richard said, 'but I've got a feeling we haven't seen the last of him. I mean, he wouldn't just give up, would he?'

Ben shrugged. 'He'll have to. He knows we've beaten him.'

'We haven't reached Manorbier yet,' Richard cautioned.

Ben opened his map out for the twentieth time. 'Look.' He pointed to Manorbier and then to Lydstep. 'Can't be more than another couple of miles.'

'Yes, but we have to find the right place in Manorbier,' Richard persisted. 'We don't really know what we're looking for, do we?'

'Oh, you are a drag,' said Ben. 'Of course we know. We've only got to mention the name Machy to someone. They'll soon direct us.'

'Direct us? To what?'

'Well, to – to – oh, I don't know!' Ben exclaimed exasperatedly. 'To whatever place they lived in, I suppose.'

'Don't you mean the place they're buried in?' queried Richard.

Ben blinked several times as he registered the correction. 'Yes,' he said lamely. He sighed. 'There is a difference, isn't there?'

The boys ate the most enormous breakfast which got rid of another four pounds-odd of their money. But they were greatly heartened by the food which they both swore was the most delicious meal they had ever eaten. Then they went to look for a telephone box. Harvesting their tenpence coins into a pile they first of all dealt with the Tenby call. They left a brief message with Mrs Powell, saying they had arrived safely and please to tell Mrs Stephens. Then they tossed up for who should phone home first. Ben won. He seemed a little embarrassed.

'Could you – um – wait outside, d'you think?' he

asked awkwardly. He was afraid the call would be an emotional one. Richard understood perfectly. He knew he would feel the same way when it was his turn.

'Hello, Mum!' Ben cried excitedly when he heard his mother's voice. 'It's me. Ben.' He heard his mother choke off a sob as she tried to keep sufficiently calm while she got the necessary information out of him. 'I'm – I mean *we're* in Wales,' Ben answered her first enquiry. 'I – I – can't tell you exactly where.' (The temptation to do so, however, was incredibly powerful.) 'We're nearly ready to come back,' he went on, hoping to reassure. 'Yes, we should be back this evening. If not, I'll ring again. Yes, we're all right.' Pause. 'Of course there's nobody with us.' Pause. 'A relation? I don't understand. We haven't any relations down here, have we?' Mrs Tompkins' question arose from the false claim made by Bone. The pips went. 'Goodbye, Mum. Don't worry,' cried Ben and hung up.

He came out of the telephone kiosk with a very sombre expression. In answer to Richard's enquiry he said, 'It was awful. My mother was so upset she could hardly speak. She was trying not to cry – oh Richard, I feel terrible.' He looked as though he was on the point of tears himself. Richard gave him a squeeze. He knew he must expect the same reaction.

However he didn't get the same reaction at all. His father answered the phone and he was very angry. He told Richard he was selfish, irresponsible and cruel. How dare he upset everyone like this? They were all worried to death. 'If you care anything for anybody other than yourself, come home at once.'

'I can't come home at once,' Richard murmured, cowed by his father's ferocity. 'I didn't mean to cause you any worry, I couldn't help it,' he said tearfully. He felt his father was unjust – he didn't understand what had driven him and Ben to leave home as they had. 'No, I'm not in Tenby.' He wouldn't admit to where they were. He heaved a sigh of relief – a shuddering sort of sigh – when the pips went and put the receiver down without even saying goodbye. He stumbled out to Ben almost in a state of shock. It was a few moments before Ben could get anything out of him.

'We – we shouldn't have done this,' he whispered at last. 'I didn't realize exactly what trouble we'd cause. I knew it was wrong to worry them, but I thought we'd only be away a day.' He looked at Ben miserably. 'Shall we go back? I'd give anything to go home.'

'So would I,' Ben concurred. 'Let's get on then. It's only a tiny bit further.'

Richard swallowed hard. 'You – you mean go on? To Manorbier? I thought you were agreeing with me to go back?'

'Oh,' said Ben. 'I see. You wanted to go *now*?'

Richard nodded.

'But we've come all this way, Rich. Why abandon our plan now? We've still got the ring and – '

'Throw it away!' Richard shouted emotionally. 'I hate the thing.'

'But, if we did, it would all start up again . . . wouldn't it?' Ben reminded him. 'Why did we come all the way if we don't care about getting nightmares and visions and – '

'Yes. Yes. All right!' Richard shouted him down through clenched teeth. 'We'll go on then. And when we get to Manorbier we'll find the spot and bury the ring. Then we'll cycle straight back to Tenby, then we'll get the train to Swansea, then the train to London, then . . .' He broke down into floods of tears. He felt frightened, angry, frustrated and isolated. Ben was alarmed. He'd never seen his friend like this. He stood helpless, completely unequipped to deal with such an outburst. After a while Richard calmed down. He gave Ben the shadow of a smile. 'Sorry,' he murmured. He re-mounted his bike. Ben did likewise. Without another word they headed off for Manorbier.

Bone, injured and outwitted by Richard, allowed his temper to cool before he began to think about his next move. He plodded back to the bus shelter and sat inside, cursing the two boys who so far had managed to stay one step ahead. He was cold, hungry and damp; his coat hadn't entirely dried out from the night before. He didn't give Mrs Stephens a thought. The fact that he was in her debt didn't register with him at all. He didn't care for people generally; his lot in life had been a hard and unlucky one, he believed, though the truth was that he was lazy, dishonest and cunning. Petty crime, as far as he was concerned, was a means to an end and so Dorothy naturally fared no better at his hands than many another person whom, in the course of his life, he had cheated or robbed.

Bone knew Richard and Ben would head for Manorbier, once their bicycles were usable again. He discovered the road they would have to take and he did consider ambushing them. But he decided against it. There were two of them, they could easily steer clear of him and he would be risking further injury to himself into the bargain. He consulted the bus timetable on the wall of the shelter. He saw that a bus ran to Penally and Lydstep and then on to Pembroke. Manorbier was off the beaten track so he would have to walk there from the nearest stop. There was a long wait before the first bus was due so he wandered off, nursing his hand, to get something to eat.

Geoffrey Bright went to work that day with a somewhat lighter heart. He scarcely noticed the crumpled body of a white cat in the gutter, the victim of a road accident. He had other things on his mind. His family at least knew Richard was unharmed and that was an enormous relief. So was the fact that Richard and Ben seemed unaware of any 'relative' travelling with them. Mr Bright regretted his outburst when it was too late. He knew Richard was in trouble and he hadn't handled the conversation with him at all well. It had been an instinctive reaction and Valerie and Ginny had never ceased to upbraid him for it in their own ways. Mrs Bright said Richard was frightened enough already without his father making it worse and Ginny said he was cruel to talk to poor Richard like that when she so wanted him to come home. He tried to alleviate his feelings of guilt by telephoning Ben's father, hoping he would perhaps understand why he had behaved as he did. But Mr Tompkins offered no support and seemed to find the other man's explanation surprising. The two families, however, were united by their concern and longing. They kept their local police informed of developments, relaying the conversations with the boys almost word for word. They were told that patrol vehicles in the Tenby area were searching for boys of Richard's and Ben's description and that they expected to receive reports that they had been found within the next few hours. The families were greatly encouraged. Meanwhile Richard and Ben reached Manorbier, a sleepy little village with an ancient ruined castle close to the bay behind which the village nestled.

The boys chained their bikes to a post in the beach car park. It was still early and there was plenty of time to find where they must take the Machy ring. They were beginning to feel their adventure was almost over and now they were drawn by the sea. It was very warm and they decided to have a paddle. Leaving their shoes and socks on the beach they splashed about gaily, refreshing themselves and relieving the anxieties of the last few hours. It was here that Donald Bone saw them as he walked past the castle at a quarter to eleven.

The first thing that entered his head as he saw them larking about was that they had disposed of the ring and were now having a boyish sort of celebration. He grimaced and clenched his fists.

'Oh, if they *have* . . .' he growled to himself, shaking his head and leaving the unspoken menace of what he would do to them hanging in the air. He saw where they had left their bikes. He wondered if this time he could do something more drastic to the machines. He looked around. Only a handful of people were out, strolling along the beach or walking the coastal path. The boys were at least a couple of hundred metres off and were oblivious of his proximity. Bone realized his arrival in Manorbier would be completely unexpected. Now he must capitalize on their lack of suspicion. Their guard was down. He strolled over to the bikes, watching Richard and Ben out of one eye as he did so. Now something told him that the ring was still in their possession. He wasn't sure why he had this feeling, but he was suddenly as certain of it as if he had been told. He seemed to see the ring bouncing up and down in a pocket as the boys, with jeans rolled up, jumped and vaulted over the little wavelets. It was strange.

Of course, he told himself, they couldn't have been in Manorbier long. So how *could* they have found where to take the ring? No, they felt safe; they were having a little interlude of fun before the serious business needed to be thought of again. All at once Bone caught sight of the footwear placed side by side on the beach with the boys' socks stuffed inside them. And alongside these were their bags. He rubbed his hands together and chuckled. This was a much better find than the bikes. He had only to bundle these things out of the boys' reach and the ring was as good as his. They would have to trade with him.

Slowly, step by step, he edged forward over the sandy beach. Richard and Ben were still in their own little world. Bone held himself tense. Now, when at last he was so close to success, he was more than ever aware just how important the ancient relic was to him. It was the key to everything. It would change his life, make his fortune, put him among the ranks of the 'haves' instead of the 'have nots' and – oh, how long he had been numbered among the latter! He mustn't slip up now. He mustn't put a foot out of place, he mustn't rush it. Oh no. Take it calmly, surreptitiously, then make that final swoop at the very last moment. He muttered to himself feverishly as he drew nearer and nearer . . . ten metres . . . six . . . three . . .

A cloud passed in front of the sun. The beach darkened. Richard and Ben ceased to play. They looked back at the beach. Ben yelled and pointed. But it was too late. Bone pounced on their belongings with an unearthly screech of triumph and, as the boys came leaping and running ashore, he bounded away across the sand, laughing and whooping like one possessed. Richard and Ben watched him in consternation. They knew the Machy ring was as good as lost.

—15—
Machy House

At the edge of the sand the boys halted. They were barefoot and the path to their bikes was rough and stony. But they were more dismayed by the sight of the despicable Bone climbing the bank to the cliff path and brandishing their shoes in front of him like a trophy.

'How on earth did he find us?' Richard wailed. 'Can't we ever escape him?'

'No good worrying about that now,' Ben said urgently. 'We've got to follow him. We must get our things back or we've really had it. We can't cycle or anything . . .'

'I know,' said Richard. 'Have you got the ring safe? That's what he wants. We'll have to bargain with him.'

Ben slapped his pocket by way of an answer. They turned and ran across the sand after the retreating thief. As they began to clamber up the grassy bank they saw up ahead of them, in the opposite direction to that taken by Bone, a grim figure. A large bearded man dressed entirely in black and wearing a top hat and black gloves beckoned to them and then pointed in the direction of the village. It was as if he was trying to tell them not to follow Bone, but to go the other way. The boys knew at once that the power of the ring was again being exerted. They were being urged, through the medium of another of the Machy apparitions, not to hand over the ring, but to finish their task and return it to its home once and for all. It was a fleeting vision that disappeared again almost at once, but the impression it made on the boys was longlasting. They felt themselves caught between two powerful impulses. They didn't know what to do.

Bone only noticed their hesitancy. He laughed and flourished their belongings at them. He saw their pale frightened faces and knew he had got them where he wanted them.

'We – we *can't* give him the ring,' Richard muttered hoarsely. 'We'd never get it back. Never. Never.'

'But we also can't walk the streets in bare feet,' Ben said in a low voice. 'We're miles from home without anyone to turn to. We'll trick him, Richard. I'm not sure how, but we must. It's our only chance.'

The friends continued upward. They reached the coastal path which, luckily for them, was fairly smooth. They kept their eyes peeled for stones or other sharp objects. Bone watched them approach. When they were about three metres away he called out harshly, 'That's far enough. Put the jewel on the ground in front of you.'

The boys looked at each other. Jewel? What did he mean? Was he referring to the stone in the ring? But it wasn't a jewel . . .

'We want our things back first,' Ben asserted.

Bone chuckled unpleasantly. 'I bet you do,' he said. 'And then you'd scarper, leaving me with nothing.' He looked about to make sure there was no one else nearby. 'No, no,' he said. 'I've got a better idea. You do what I say. Otherwise you won't see these again.' And he swept his arm round as though he was going to hurl the boys' shoes into the sea.

'Stop! Wait!' cried Richard who really thought he was going to let them go. Bone brought his arm back. 'Ben, we've got no choice,' Richard said to his friend.

Ben put his hand in his pocket and slowly drew the
ring out. He held it at arm's length so that Bone could
see there was no trick. The man nodded. 'That's right.
Now put it down. There.' He indicated a spot half-way
between them.

'I'll put it there if you put our socks and trainers next
to it,' said Ben. 'So that we can make the exchange
simultaneously.' He nudged Richard. If they were quick
they might be able to grab the whole lot back. But Bone
was no fool. He saw the nudge and guessed exactly what
they were planning.

'I can't quite agree to that,' he told them. 'But I don't
want to be unreasonable. So I'll put two shoes down
when I see that jewel on the ground. O.K.? Then, when
I have it in my hand I'll put the others down.'

The boys were in no position to argue. But they both
thought that, with one pair of shoes returned, one of
them could still snatch the ring back and run to the
village. The only problem was, whose shoes would they
be? However, here again Bone made sure he wasn't
fooled. As Ben laid the ring on the grass beside the path
the man, with a cunning grin, set two left shoes down
by its side. The boys' faces dropped. Bone laughed.
Then he stretched out his empty hand to take the ring.
As his fingers just touched it a dark figure suddenly
loomed up behind the boys on the cliff path. Bone hadn't
seen the figure approach. It was again a bearded man
in a top hat who gestured angrily and pointed towards
the village in an imperious manner. Ben and Richard
were unaware of the figure's reappearance but they saw
Bone gape and pause, his fingers still stretched out.

'Grab the ring!' Richard hissed and, at the same
instant, leapt forward at the unsuspecting Bone who was
leaning forward and off balance. Richard pushed hard
at him with both arms. Bone slipped and fell backward.

Ben snatched the ring and the shoes on the ground.
Richard wrested the other shoes from the startled man's
grip and together the boys danced away, gleefully clutching their belongings and then ran helter-skelter down
the bank to the sand. Then across the beach they went,
still barefoot, running like the wind. Turning at the path
to the bikes they stopped momentarily and hopped first
on one leg, then the other as they tugged their trainers
on. They didn't bother to lace them and they shoved
their socks into their pockets as they raced to retrieve
their bags from the beach. Bone's fury at once again
being outwitted knew no bounds and, heedless of
onlookers, he charged down the bank roaring with rage.

The boys darted back over the sand, sprinting to their
bikes. They knew Bone would try and head them off
and, out of sheer desperation, they now ran harder then
ever. They slipped the chains off their bikes and swung
their legs over just as Bone came pounding towards
them.

'Head for the village,' yelled Richard, 'and then keep
going. We'll put a stretch between us.'

They pedalled furiously away, excited and exhilarated
by their success. They felt that Bone could never stop
them now and they whooped in derision at the man who
was vainly shaking his fist at them from the car park.

'We've got to hole up somewhere,' Richard gasped as
they struggled uphill. 'We have to have – a place to
hide. Till it's – dark.'

Manorbier itself wasn't safe. They left the village
behind and set their bikes in the direction of Pembroke.
A police car passed them on the other side of the road
and, a short distance further on, came to a halt. Richard
and Ben barely noticed it and, on their side of the road,
round a bend, they presently came to an old manor
house, set in huge wild grounds and surrounded by an

ancient stone wall. The whole place looked neglected, careworn and wonderfully secluded. Richard recognized its possibilities instantly.

'In here,' he cried. There was no evidence yet of their pursuer, yet both boys had cause to know just how determined Bone was. He was as relentless as a bloodhound. They rode their bikes up a weed-strewn path and into a dark overgrown laurel shrubbery at the side of the house. There was a dead bird, a house-martin, lying on the path. They both stared at it.

'That reminds me of old Mackie's house,' said Ben and then he clapped a hand to his mouth. He saw Richard's expression. They shared the same thought. *Could* it be? *Was* it possible? They both had a strange feeling. The omen!

'There's a link,' Richard whispered. 'I can sort of sense it.'

Ben nodded vigorously. 'So can I,' he said. 'We were drawn here.'

The sound of a police siren made their attention wander but only for a moment or two until it disappeared into the distance.

'We'd better wait for a bit,' said Richard. 'Lie low in here.' They were well hidden in the vegetation. 'I wouldn't be a bit surprised if Bone suddenly wandered in. It's uncanny how he tracks us.'

Actually they were quite safe. Bone was combing Manorbier village for them at that juncture, stone by stone. The boys were itching to explore. They looked at their watches. It was still only just past noon. They shared their last can of drink and then thoughtfully replaced their socks.

After an hour or so they were both extremely fidgety. Ben was all for investigating the empty house but Richard was more cautious. 'The minute we step into the open Bone will appear, I just know it,' he said.

Ben swatted a gnat. The shrubbery was rich in troublesome insects. 'I think if he was going to come he would have been here by now,' he grumbled. He was having the worst of the encounters with the insects.

'Let's have something to eat,' Richard suggested as a diversion.

'We've only got tinned stuff,' Ben reminded him.

'Well, that's all right.' Richard began pulling hot-dog sausages and baked beans out of his bag. 'Oh dear,' he muttered. 'I don't think I brought a tin opener.'

'Trust you,' Ben grunted. '*I've* got one.' He sought for it in his own bag and, in the process, fished out some tinned peaches and a spoon. He opened the sausages and beans. The boys took turns in dipping into the tins.

'Didn't know cold baked beans could taste so nice,' said Richard afterwards while Ben exposed the contents of the can of fruit. The meal passed another fifteen minutes or so.

Ben got stickier and itchier. 'Oh, *come* on, Rich,' he said at length. 'We can't stay in here for ever. Let's creep round the back – we'd be hidden there anyway.'

Richard shrugged. Ben took it as a sign of agreement and led the way out of the shrubbery. The main entrance to the house was at the side. There was a broad and lofty porch and a flight of stone steps leading up to it. There was a coat of arms carved over the stone doorway. It seemed familiar. Then Ben grabbed Richard's arm and squeezed painfully in his excitement. On the stone lintel over the door was carved in old lettering: 'Machy House'.

'Phew!' Ben exhaled a long sigh. 'We've made it!'

Richard gave a joyful little jump. 'I knew this was it,' he said.

They crept through the weeds around to the back of the house. Here was what once had been a magnificent terraced garden with tall hedges and long sloping lawns with colourful beds of roses and massed flowers that even now struggled to bloom amongst the choking undergrowth. But the boys were more interested in the house itself. They went up to the tall latticed windows, shading their eyes to look in. The house was a shell. It had been cleared long ago, quite unlike the House of the Martins where rooms were filled with every conceivable object. The only evidence that Machy House had ever been inhabited were the great deep stone fireplaces. Here the blackened hearths remained as reminders of days of company, warmth, bustle, conversation by roaring log fires: the old life that once had been lived inside the enduring stone walls.

Ben and Richard were disappointed. 'Dead,' said Ben. 'A house of the dead. The family died out and this is all that's left of them.'

'It seems sad,' Richard remarked, 'the house, I mean. Sad and forlorn here on its own with no one to use it. I wonder what will happen?'

'It'll be sold like the other house in Hallenden, I should think,' Ben said. 'Or pulled down. It's too big for anyone to want to live in it now.'

'No wonder old Mackie preferred to live elsewhere,' Richard observed. Then he was struck by a thought. 'Ben, he couldn't have been brought here, could he? You know – afterwards.'

'What for?' Ben queried. 'There's no graveyard around here.'

'No, but it's his ancestral home. Perhaps he wanted to be returned to lie among his forebears. Some of these old houses used to have vaults.'

Ben shuddered. 'I don't fancy searching for that,' he

said. 'A bit spooky, don't you think? And if there is a burial vault where all the generations were laid to rest, I reckon there would be more risk of seeing phantoms there than ever before. They might all rise up together if we threatened to disturb them.' He was frightening himself.

'Don't be silly,' said Richard sharply. 'We don't want to disturb anything. Quite the opposite. We've brought the ring to them, all this way, to pacify them. I think we should search for their tombs here and leave their heirloom amongst them where it'll be safe for ever.'

'Blow that,' said Ben. '*You* can, if you like. How do you know they're not all buried in Manorbier church-yard? We didn't even look.'

'Well, we're here now, aren't we? So we can look here first.'

'*You* can, you mean.'

'All right,' said Richard calmly. 'Give me the ring. I want to get this business over and get home. What do you want to do?'

Ben shrugged. 'The same, of course.' He saw there was no help for it. 'Oh, very well then,' he said reluctantly. 'If we must, let's get on with it before ghastly Bone turns up again.'

Richard smiled. 'Good old Ben,' he said warmly. 'I knew you would.'

'Where do we start?'

'Well, a vault would be under the house, wouldn't it? So let's walk round and see if there's any sign of an entrance from outside.'

They crept round the entire building, searching all four sides and sometimes trampling down weeds and squeezing through overgrown shrubs to do so. They found nothing.

'Perhaps the entrance is from the inside,' said Richard as they got back to their starting point.

'Oh look, we don't even know if there *is* a vault,' said Ben irritably. 'Why on earth can't we go and look at the church in Manorbier?'

'It wouldn't be safe until it's dark,' Richard pointed out. 'We'd be discovered in no time in the daylight. He must be frantically searching for us at this moment.'

'You're very comforting,' Ben observed sarcastically.

'Sorry, Ben,' said Richard ruefully. 'I didn't intend to worry you. I tell you what. You wait here somewhere. I'm going to look in all the windows this time – we missed quite a lot at the front and on one side. There just might be a clue in one of the rooms.'

Ben was perfectly happy with this arrangement. He installed himself on a stone balustrade in the sun, overlooking the terraced garden. Richard began his investigation.

The afternoon sun was very hot. Ben drooped, then nodded . . . suddenly he was awake again. Richard was shaking him excitedly. 'Come and see, come and see,' he babbled, 'you'll never guess what I've found.'

'What?' Ben grunted sleepily.

'A chapel! One of the rooms was used as a chapel. And there are steps down from it underneath. There must be a crypt. That's where they're buried, the whole lot of them.'

Ben couldn't raise much enthusiasm. 'So what?'

'So that's where we put the ring, dopey. Then we can leave.'

'How do we get into the house?' Ben wanted to know.

'Through a window, of course.'

'You mean there's a window open?' Ben asked, astonished.

'No, no. How could there be? We'll have to break one.'

'We can't do that!'

'Why not? We have to.'

'It's not our property; it'd be vandalism.'

'Only one small pane, you know, one of those little diamond shaped ones, so that I can put my hand in and open the latch.'

Ben pursed his lips. 'I don't know, Richard,' he said doubtfully.

'Who's to know?' Richard said.

Ben giggled. 'Only the Machys,' he answered.

'And they want this back.' Richard held the old relic up to the light as if signalling to all the long-dead antecedents of Mr Mackie that here was the thing they craved and that he – Richard – was the agent linking them to its restoration.

'All right,' said Ben nervously, 'enough of the dramatics.' He looked round to make sure a whole fleet of ghosts hadn't been roused by the gesture. 'Let's see this chapel.'

Richard led him to the far side of the house. Ben gazed in at the simple altar, the few pews divided by an aisle, and one single painting of what he assumed was a saint. Then he saw the steps. 'It's dark in there, I can't make out what's at the bottom but it looks like a metal grille. I'll go and get my torch.' Meanwhile Richard was hunting for a rock or a big stone with which to smash the pane.

When Ben returned Richard had made a hole. His hand was still swathed in the handkerchief he had used to protect it, and he was clinging on to the wall with one hand and trying to heave himself up with the other by grasping the sill through the broken pane.

'Hold on,' said Ben. 'I'll help you.' He bent double.

'Climb on my back,' he offered. Richard did so and from this raised position was easily able to reach the latch and swing the rusty window open. The first fresh air for many a year, he supposed, blew into the musty chapel. Richard climbed over the sill and dropped to the floor.

'Hand me your torch,' he ordered. Ben obliged. Richard went carefully down the narrow steps as Ben peered in at him. He switched the torch on. Presently Ben heard a rattle followed by a moan. 'Oh no!' Richard groaned. 'There's a metal grating here and it's locked.'

'What's inside?' Ben called.

There was a moment's silence as Richard swept the torch around. 'Tombs,' he whispered. 'Stone coffins on raised platforms. And metal plaques on the wall. They're all Machys. There are scores of them. This is what we've been searching for all along, Ben, and we can't get into it!'

— 16 —
The Reclaiming of the Ring

The boys were stumped. They were so near and yet so far. Without much enthusiasm Ben said, 'Couldn't you just fling the ring through the grating? It'd still be among them, wouldn't it?'

Richard remounted the steps. 'No,' he said. 'What would be the good of that? Supposing the house *is* knocked down some time? And, even if it isn't, the ring would be too easy to find by someone like Bone if it landed where it could easily be seen. It has to be hidden. Don't you see?'

Ben did. He nodded gloomily. He watched Richard climb out of the chapel and relatch the window. 'Now what?'

'Well,' said Richard, 'we'll simply have to search around the house for a place to hide the ring in.'

'What, you mean a crack in the wall, something like that?'

'Not exactly, but that sort of thing, I suppose.'

'Let's begin at the front, then. Perhaps there's somewhere under the porch.'

'Good idea.'

While they were examining the stone steps and the

porch itself they noticed something they had missed before. There was a dark blue sticker adhering to a panel on the front door. It had seemed insignificant and they had overlooked it earlier. But now they were searching every crevice, every feature, they couldn't help but read it. The sticker proclaimed: 'HOUSE AND LANDS PURCHASED BY S.P.H.W.B. with funds raised entirely by private donations.' It was a simple unexciting-looking sticker, but when the friends looked closer they saw that the initials stood for 'The Society for the Preservation of Historic Welsh Buildings' and they realized the importance of their discovery.

'It's the answer to everything!' Richard cried jubilantly. 'The house is saved, and so are we. It means we can bury the ring in the grounds. It'll be preserved for ever then in its true home, as long as we bury it deep.'

' "S.P.H.W.B.",' quoted Ben. His memory dredged up something from the very beginning of their adventure. 'Do you think that was the charity that old Mackie willed his money to?'

Richard slapped him on the back. 'Of course! You're brilliant!' he congratulated him. He hadn't made the connection himself. 'Everything falls into place. He wanted the ancestral home to be saved, otherwise it would have been sold like his house in Hallenden. And all the proceeds from *that* place will help to pay for this one. Oh, it's perfect, Ben.'

The boys celebrated, dancing round and round with their arms entwined. They decided to bury the Machy ring in the rose garden; then they had second thoughts. Richard said, 'If the charity has bought the whole place, the gardens will be restored, you know. There'll be visitors. And gardeners might unearth the relic.'

'What about the lawn?' Ben suggested. 'They wouldn't be likely to dig there.'

'Oh Ben, you're super-ace! It'd be the most wonderful spot of all. Now what we need is something to dig with. I bet there's an old shed somewhere with tools in. Come on, let's have a hunt round.'

Bone soon discovered his quarry was nowhere in the village. Cursing and swearing at the boys' tactics he left Manorbier and reached the cross-roads where he looked left to Pembroke and right to the Tenby road. Which road had they taken? His unerring instinct for tracking Richard and Ben once again served him well. He didn't think the boys would have doubled back to Tenby. He knew what they were searching for and he guessed they wouldn't give up now they were so near their goal. Consequently he turned into the direction of Pembroke.

Of course the boys had lost some of their caution. They had hidden their bikes, but were no longer so careful about themselves. At the time they were leaping about in delight at the discovery of the blue sticker Bone paused at the entrance to Machy House, attracted by a flash of movement. He crept stealthily along the drive and there, by the front porch, were the two young people he had trailed for so long. He almost hugged himself with glee. But he quickly smothered the impulse. He needed to be cool and collected. He would need all his wits about him if he were to prise the jewel from the boys' grasp at this late stage. He must follow their every movement and, above all, not arouse their suspicion.

He saw them run to the back of the house. He crept after them. He saw the name 'Machy House' over the threshold and knew the boys had reached the end of their journey. He crept round the house. Ben and Richard were searching the grounds for the elusive digging tool. Bone secreted himself behind a leafy bush and viewed their proceedings. He longed to make a rush at them and wrest the ring from their possession but he didn't know which of them was carrying it, and he had to accept that two healthy young boys could once again prove his match. He needed to be patient and wait for the right moment; then make sure of it once and for all.

There was no shed and there were no tools of any description to be found. 'Looking at this garden, I wonder if there ever were any?' Ben joked feebly.

The boys strolled on to the lawn. It was soft and damp from last night's downpour. 'You know,' Ben went on more practically, 'it wouldn't take very much to make a hole here, it's so spongy. If we could find a stout stick and make a point on it we could drive that into the grass. That would make a very neat hole.'

They lost no time in following up his sensible suggestion. And now Richard came up trumps. 'Let's look in the flower beds,' he said. 'There may be some stakes amongst the plants.'

They went systematically along the borders, blissfully unaware of the onlooker. They had all but forgotten Bone. They came to a clump of straggly lupins. A rusty metal rod once used as a stake, could still be seen amongst the foliage. It was ideal for their purposes. It was even sharp at one end. They tugged it up and ran back to the lawn. They pushed the stake into the grass. Ben found a large stone which they used as a mallet. The metal rod made a beautifully deep and narrow hole. They knocked it down almost to its entire length, about a metre and a half. Then they wrenched it up again. The boys got down on their knees and took turns in squinting down the hole. Of course they couldn't see anything.

'That should do it,' Ben pronounced.

'I should think so,' Richard agreed. He took the ring from his pocket.

Behind the bush Bone watched, tense but absorbed with the boys' actions. He had entirely forgotten the black figure on the cliffside, the appearance of which had been so brief he had dismissed it as a figment of his own imagination.

Richard held the ring in his palm. The object that had caused the boys so much trouble and anxiety was at last about to be released from their grasp and consigned to a spot where they could no longer reach it. In a moment it would be returned to the ancestral soil of its real and historic owners.

'It's farewell to the ring,' Richard said simply and dropped it down into the cylindrical hole. Then he pushed the metal stake in again to make sure the relic reached the very bottom. The boys stamped the grass down around the hole and soon there was barely any sign that the overgrown lawn had been disturbed.

They both felt an overwhelming sense of relief. The spell of the ring had been broken and now they could carry on with their normal lives. As long as the Machy heirloom remained buried in Machy ground they would have achieved their aim and, in addition, the ill luck associated with its possession by anyone other than a Machy could not be resurrected. Ben and Richard were sure they had made the ring safe but they hadn't reckoned with Donald Bone. The boys' one thought was to set off for home without any further delay. They ran towards the house excited by the prospect. They thought their ordeal was finally over and they longed to be reunited with their families. As they ran one way Bone darted from hiding and ran in the opposite direction, straight to the lawn. The friends were startled by his sudden appearance and skidded to a halt. They could scarcely believe what they saw.

'It's – it's not possible,' Richard muttered. 'Where could he have come from? How could he have found us?'

'He must have been here all the time in secret,' Ben said with a sort of revulsion. 'He's seen everything!'

They couldn't bear to think all their efforts had been in vain and now, at the moment of their final release, to have everything spoilt by this hateful man who dogged them every step of the way. It was just too much for them. Sobbing with frustration and anger, Richard managed to blurt out, 'We've got to stop him, Ben!'

Ben was ready. Neither of the boys was prepared to allow Bone to wreck their plan and together they rushed at him, yelling at him to get away. They hadn't had time to think properly what they could do but they were both determined he shouldn't succeed. And now help from an unexpected source was at hand.

Bone had snatched up the metal rod and was probing the ground in order to locate the hole only just covered by Richard and Ben's foot-work. The rod slipped into the mark it had made and Bone, ramming it down, actually heard the 'chink' as the rod's end struck the ring. He laughed at the boys' shouts and hauled the rod out again. But his mirth was short-lived. In striking the ring he had disturbed a power more ancient even than the thing he sought. As Bone began to dig divots of grass and soil from the ground, using the rod as a makeshift fork, a dark cloud seemed to materialize from the earth itself. It was so strange that Ben and Richard's headlong charge was stalled. Fascinated but afraid they halted only a metre to two from the edge of the lawn, and stood gaping at the phenomenon. The cloud began to take shape and the boys, terrified but unable to move, saw it assume the shape of a man – a huge man, a giant; dark and sombre-looking with long lank hair that brushed his chest, and with a great black beard. The figure wore a black robe pinned at the shoulder by a gold brooch. His other clothing was obscured but his enormous muscular legs were quite bare. It was a primitive figure, a mighty figure and, as Bone reeled, fell back before it, it raised one huge arm and stretched forth its open left hand, as broad as a dinner-plate, towards him. There, miraculously, on the third finger the boys and their persecutor saw the Machy ring and now they knew this phantom was none other than Cawr y Cewri, the great Welsh prince himself, the forefather of the entire Machy race.

Bone crumpled before the phantom like an empty sack and cowered, whimpering, as if awaiting his awful sentence. But, as suddenly as it had appeared, the dread figure vanished, leaving no trace. The boys took a while before they could regain their senses and neither were able to speak. As for Bone, when the image's power released him from its sway, he stumbled to his feet and ran shrieking and without a backward glance towards the front of the house. The Machy ring had been, as it were, snatched back before his very eyes by its original and only wearer.

Slowly Richard and Ben recovered themselves. White-faced but somehow enthralled by their experience, they silently turned away from the place that now and for ever had reclaimed its own.

Conclusion

Bone's flight took him only as far as the front garden where he ran slap into a hefty Welsh police officer. The police car which earlier had passed the boys on their bikes had patrolled the immediate area and, by a process of elimination, the officers had narrowed their search to the only place where the boys could have hidden themselves, namely the grounds of Machy House.

After Dorothy Stephens' information about Bone had been passed to them, the man had been wanted for questioning about his alleged intrusion into the boys' bedroom while under her roof. There was also the lesser offence of non-payment for his own accommodation there. He was hauled away before he could understand what was happening to him and, very soon afterwards, the boys showed themselves and were asked some preliminary questions by the police merely to confirm that they were the two missing English boys from Hallenden. Then they were taken into police care, bikes included, while the respective families were informed.

At the local police station they were able to give an account to the police about the episode in the bedroom. They couldn't think why anyone would be bothered about it but they answered the questions faithfully and the officers seemed satisfied. The boys also informed the police that Donald Bone was a thief, describing the House of the Martins at Hallenden and what they thought he had removed from it. They were a little embarrassed when they were asked how they themselves had such an intimate knowledge of the place but they answered truthfully and their questioners were more amused by their answers than anything else. The information about Bone's burglaries was passed to the police in Hallenden. The boys were able to have a wash and they were given sandwiches and coffee. They were allowed to speak to their parents on the telephone and they rather began to enjoy themselves. The Machy ring, its power, and the visions it invoked were not of much interest to the police force except insofar as it explained the reason for the boys' journey to Wales. Boys' vivid imaginations, they concluded, were at the root of it all.

Richard and Ben didn't see Bone again. They were driven to Tenby station along the selfsame route they themselves had cycled. As they passed Machy House Ben gave a muffled exclamation. He dug Richard in the ribs. 'Look!' he hissed. 'Isn't that the white cat?'

Richard, though, was tired of phantoms and visions. The adventure was over and they were going home. He did see a white blur but he only said in answer to Ben, 'How could it be? The animal couldn't come here by itself. And we don't have the ring any more so it wasn't a phantom. You must have been mistaken.' His mind returned to other things. The entire Bright and Tompkins families were to meet them at Paddington and Richard was looking forward to the inevitable hugs and embraces. He couldn't help wondering if he might even be lucky enough to get a kiss from Angela.